George Gissing

The Emancipated - A Novel

Vol. I

George Gissing

The Emancipated - A Novel
Vol. I

ISBN/EAN: 9783337031428

Printed in Europe, USA, Canada, Australia, Japan

Cover: Foto ©Andreas Hilbeck / pixelio.de

More available books at **www.hansebooks.com**

THE EMANCIPATED

A Novel

BY

GEORGE GISSING

AUTHOR OF "THE NETHER WORLD," "THYRZA," ETC.

IN THREE VOLUMES.

VOL. I.

LONDON:

RICHARD BENTLEY AND SON,

Publishers in Ordinary to Her Majesty the Queen.

1890.

CONTENTS OF VOL. I.

———◦◦◦———

PART I.

PART I.

THE EMANCIPATED.

CHAPTER I.

NORTHERNERS IN SUNLIGHT.

By a window looking from Posilipo upon
the Bay of Naples sat an English lady,
engaged in letter-writing. She was not
more than four and twenty, but her attire
of subdued mourning indicated widowhood
already at the stage when it is permitted
to make quiet suggestion of freedom rather
than distressful reference to loss; the dress,
however, was severely simple, and its grey
coldness, which would well have harmonized
with an English sky in this month of
November, looked alien in the southern
sunlight. There was no mistaking her

nationality; the absorption, the troubled
earnestness with which she bent over her
writing, were peculiar to a cast of features
such as can be found only in our familiar
island; a physiognomy not quite pure
in outline, vigorous in general effect and
in detail delicate; a proud young face,
full of character and capacity, beautiful
in chaste control. Sorrowful it was not,
but its paleness and thinness expressed
something more than imperfect health of
body; the blue-grey eyes, when they
wandered for a moment in an effort of
recollection, had a look of weariness, even
of ennui; the lips moved as if in nervous
impatience until she had found the phrase
or the thought for which her pen waited.
Save for these intervals, she wrote with
quick decision, in a large clear hand, never
underlining, but frequently supplying the
emphasis of heavy stroke in her penning of a
word. At the end of her letters came a signature excellent in individuality: "Miriam
Baske."

The furniture of her room was modern, and of the kind demanded by wealthy *forestieri* in the lodgings they condescend to occupy. On the variegated tiles of the floor were strewn rugs and carpets; the drapery was bright, without much reference to taste in the ordering of hues; a handsome stove served at present to support leafy plants, a row of which also stood on the balcony before the window. Round the ceiling ran a painted border of foliage and flowers. The chief ornament of the walls was a large and indifferent copy of Raphael's "St. Cecilia;" there were, too, several *gouache* drawings of local scenery, a fiery night-view of Vesuvius, a panorama of the bay, and a very blue Blue Grotto. The whole was blithe, sunny, Neapolitan; sufficiently unlike a sitting-room in Redbeck House, Bartles, Lancashire, which Mrs. Baske often had in mind as she wrote.

A few English books lay here and there, volumes of unattractive binding, and presenting titles little suggestive of a holiday

in Campania; works which it would be
misleading to call theological; the feeblest
modern echoes of fierce old Puritans, half
shame-faced modifications of logic which,
at all events, was wont to conceal no consequence of its savage premises. More
noticeable were some architectural plans
unrolled upon a settee; the uppermost
represented the elevation of a building
designed for religious purposes, painfully
recognizable by all who know the con-
venticles of sectarian England. On the
blank space beneath the drawing were a
few comments, lightly pencilled.

Having finished and addressed some half
a dozen brief letters, Mrs. Baske brooded
for several minutes before she began to
write on the next sheet of paper. It was
intended for her sister-in-law, a lady of
middle age, who shared in the occupancy
of Redbeck House. At length she penned
the introductory formula, but again became
absent, and sat gazing at the branches of
a pine-tree which stood in strong relief

against cloudless blue. A sigh, an impatient gesture, and she went on with her task.

"It is very kind of you to be so active in attending to the things which you know I have at heart. You say I shall find everything as I could wish it on my return, but you cannot think what a stranger to Bartles I already feel. It will soon be six months since I lived my real life there; during my illness I might as well have been absent, then came those weeks in the Isle of Wight, and now this exile. I feel it as exile, bitterly. To be sure Naples is beautiful, but it does not interest me. You need not envy me the bright sky, for it gives me no pleasure. There is so much to pain and sadden; so much that makes me angry. On Sunday I was miserable. The Spences are as kind as any one could be, but—— I won't write about it; no doubt you understand me.

"What do you think ought to be done about Mrs. Ackworth and her daughter? It is shameful, after all they have received from me. Will you tell them that I am gravely displeased to hear of their absenting themselves from chapel. I have a very good mind to write to Mr. Higginson and beg him to suspend the girl from his employment until she becomes regular in her attendance at worship. Perhaps that would seem malicious, but she and her mother ought to be punished in some way. Speak to them very sternly.

"I do not understand how young Brooks has dared to tell you I promised him work in the greenhouse. He is irreclaimable; the worst character that ever came under my notice; he shall not set foot on the premises. If he is in want, he has only himself to blame. I do not like to think of his wife suffering, but it is the attribute of sins such as his that they involve the innocent with the guilty; and then she has shown herself so wretchedly weak. Try, however, to help her secretly if her distress becomes too acute.

"It was impertinent in Mrs. Walker to

make such reference to me in public. This is the result of my absence and helplessness. I shall write to her—two lines."

A flush had risen to her cheek, and in adding the last two words she all but pierced through the thin note-paper. Then her hand trembled so much that she was obliged to pause. At the same moment there sounded a tap at the door, and, on Mrs. Baske's giving permission, a lady entered. This was Mrs. Spence, a cousin of the young widow; she and her husband had an apartment here in the Villa Sannazao, and were able to devote certain rooms to the convenience of their relative during her stay at Naples. Her age was about thirty; she had a graceful figure, a manner of much refinement, and a bright, gentle, intellectual face, which just now bore an announcement of news.

" They have arrived ! "

" Already ? " replied the other, in a tone of civil interest.

" They decided not to break the journey

after Genoa. Cecily and Mrs. Lessingham
are too tired to do anything but get settled
in their rooms, but Mr. Mallard has come to
tell us."

Miriam laid down her pen, and asked in
the same voice as before :

" Shall I come ? "

" If you are not too busy." And Mrs.
Spence added, with a smile, " I should think
you must have a certain curiosity to see
each other, after so long an acquaintance at
second-hand."

" I will come in a moment."

Mrs. Spence left the room. For a minute
Miriam sat reflecting, then rose. In moving
towards the door she chanced to see her
image in a mirror—two of large size adorned
the room—and it checked her step; she
regarded herself gravely, and passed a
smoothing hand over the dark hair above
her temples.

By a corridor she reached her friends'
sitting-room, where Mrs. Spence sat in the
company of two gentlemen. The elder of

these was Edward Spence. His bearded face, studious of cast and small-featured, spoke a placid, self-commanding character; a lingering smile, and the pleasant wrinkles about his brow, told of a mind familiar with many by-ways of fancy and reflection. His companion, a man of five and thirty, had a far more striking countenance. His complexion was of the kind which used to be called adust—burnt up with inner fires; his visage was long and somewhat harshly designed, very apt, it would seem, to the expression of bitter ironics or stern resentments, but at present bright with friendly pleasure. He had a heavy moustache, but no beard; his hair tumbled in disorder. To matters of costume he evidently gave little thought, for his clothes, though of the kind a gentleman would wear in travelling, had seen their best days, and the waistcoat even lacked one of its buttons; his black necktie was knotted into an indescribable shape, and the ends hung loose.

Him Mrs. Spence at once presented to

her cousin as " Mr. Mallard." He bowed
ungracefully; then, with a manner naturally
frank but constrained by obvious shyness,
took the hand Miriam held to him.

" We are scarcely strangers, Mr. Mallard," she said in a self-possessed tone,
regarding him with steady eyes.

" Miss Doran has spoken of you frequently on the journey," he replied, knitting
his brows into a scowl as he smiled and
returned her look. " Your illness made
her very anxious. You are much better,
I hope ? "

" Much, thank you."

Allowance made for the difference of
quality in their voices, Mrs. Baske and
Mallard resembled each other in speech.
They had the same grave note, the same
decision.

" They must be very tired after their
journey," Miriam added, seating herself.

" Miss Doran seems scarcely so at all ;
but Mrs. Lessingham is rather over-
wearied, I'm afraid."

"Why didn't you break the journey at Florence or Rome?" asked Mrs. Spence.

"I proposed it, but other counsels prevailed. All through Italy Miss Doran was distracted between desire to get to Naples and misery at not being able to see the towns we passed. At last she buried herself in the 'Revue des Deux Mondes,' and refused even to look out of the window."

"I suppose we may go and see her in the morning?" said Miriam.

"My express instructions are," replied Mallard, "that you are on no account to go. They will come here quite early. Miss Doran begged hard to come with me now, but I wouldn't allow it."

"Is it the one instance in which your authority has prevailed?" inquired Spence. "You seem to declare it in a tone of triumph."

"Well," replied the other, with a grim smile, leaning forward in his chair, "I don't undertake to lay down rules for the young lady of eighteen as I could for the child of twelve. But my age and sobriety of character still ensure me respect."

He glanced at Mrs. Baske, and their eyes met. Miriam smiled rather coldly, but continued to observe him after he had looked away again.

"You met them at Genoa?" she asked presently, in her tone of habitual reserve.

"Yes. I came by sea from London, and had a couple of days to wait for their arrival from Paris."

"And I suppose you also are staying at Madame Glück's?"

"Oh no! I have a room at old quarters of mine high up in the town, Vico Bran caccio. I shall only be in Naples a few days."

"How's that?" inquired Spence.

"I'm going to work at Amalfi and Paestum."

"Then, as usual, we shall see nothing of you," said Mrs. Spence. "Pray, do you dine at Madame Glück's this evening?"

"By no means."

"May we, then, have the pleasure of your company? There is no need to go back to Vico Brancaccio. I am sure Mrs. Baske will excuse you the torture of uniform."

With a sort of grumble, the invitation was accepted. A little while after, Spence proposed to his friend a walk before sunset.

"Yes; let us go up the hill," said Mallard, rising abruptly. "I need movement after the railway."

They left the villa, and Mallard grew less restrained in his conversation.

"How does Mrs. Baske answer to your expectations?" Spence asked him.

"I had seen her photograph, you know."

"Where?"

"Her brother showed it me—one taken at the time of her marriage."

"What is Elgar doing at present?"

"It's more than a year since we crossed each other," Mallard replied. "He was then going to the devil as speedily as can in reason be expected of a man. I happened to encounter him one morning at Victoria Station, and he seemed to have just slept off a great deal of heavy drinking. Told me he was going down to Brighton to see about selling a houseful of furniture there—his own property. I didn't inquire how or why he came possessed of it. The youth is beyond help, I imagine. When he comes to his last penny, he'll probably blow his brains out; just the fellow to do that kind of thing."

"I suppose he hasn't done it already? His sister has heard nothing of him for two years at least, and this account of yours is the latest I have received."

"I should think he still lives. He would be sure to make a *coup de théâtre* of his exit."

"Poor lad!" said the elder man, with feeling. "I liked him."

"Why, so did I; and I wish it had been in my scope to keep him in some kind of order. Yes, I liked him much. And as for brains, why, I have scarcely known a man who so impressed me with a sense of

his ability.   But you could see that he was
doomed from his cradle.   Strongly like his
sister in face."

"I'm afraid the thought of him troubles
her a good deal."

"She looks ill."

"Yes; we are uneasy about her," said
Spence.   Then, with a burst of impatience,
"There's no getting her mind away from
that pestilent Bartles.   What do you think
she is projecting now ?   It appears that
the Dissenters of Bartles are troubled concerning their chapel; it isn't large enough.
So Miriam proposes to pull down her own
house, and build them a chapel on the site,
of course at her own expense.   The ground
being her freehold, she can unfortunately
do what she likes with it; the same with
her personal property.   The thing has gone
so far that a Manchester firm of architects
have prepared plans; they are lying about
in her room here."

Mallard regarded the speaker with humorous wonder.

" And the fact is," pursued Spence, " that such an undertaking as this will impoverish her. She is not so wealthy as to be able to lay out thousands of pounds and leave her position unaltered."

"I suppose she lives only for her religious convictions ? "

" I don't profess to understand her. Her character is not easily sounded. But no doubt she has the puritanical spirit in a rather rare degree. I daily thank the fates that my wife grew up apart from that branch of the family. Of all the accursed——— But this is an old topic ; better not to heat one's self uselessly."

" A Puritan at Naples," mused Mallard. " The situation is interesting."

" Very. But then she doesn't really live in Naples. From the first day she has shown herself bent on resisting every influence of the place. She won't admit that the climate benefits her ; she won't allow an expression of interest in anything Italian to escape her. I doubt whether we shall ever

get her even to Pompeii. One afternoon I
persuaded her to walk up here with me,
and tried to make her confess that this view
was beautiful. She grudged making any
such admission. It is her nature to *distrust*
the beautiful."

"To be sure. That is the badge of her
persuasion."

"Last Sunday we didn't know whether
to compassionate her or to be angry with
her. The Bradshaws are at Madame Glück's.
You know them by name, I think? There
again, an interesting study, in a very different way. Twice in the day she shut
herself up with them in their rooms, and
they held a dissident service. The hours
she spent here were passed in the solitude
of her own room, lest she should witness
our profane enjoyment of the fine weather.
Eleanor refrained from touching the piano,
and at meals kept the gravest countenance,
in mere kindness. I doubt whether that
is right. It isn't as though we were dealing
with a woman whose mind is hopelessly—

immatured; she is only a girl still, and I
know she has brains if she could be induced
to use them."

"Mrs. Baske has a remarkable face, it
seems to me," said Mallard.

"It enrages me to talk of the matter."

They were now on the road which runs
along the ridge of Posilipo; at a point
where it is parted only by a low wall from
the westward declivity, they paused and
looked towards the setting sun.

"What a noise from Fuorigrotta!" murmured Spence, when he had leaned for a
moment on the wall. "It always amuses
me. Only in this part of the world could
so small a place make such a clamour."

The scene that spread before them was of
the kind it is idle to describe in words, and
yet, if only for the glory and sweetness of
the names, I cannot but touch its outlines.
They were looking away from Naples. At
the foot of the vine-covered hillside lay the
noisy village, or suburb, named from its
position at the outer end of the tunnel

which the Romans pierced to make a shorter
way between Naples and Puteoli; thence
stretched an extensive plain, set in a deep
amphitheatre of hills, and terminated by the
sea. Vineyards and maizefields, pine-trees
and poplars, diversify its surface, and through
the midst of it runs a long, straight road,
dwindling till it reaches the shore at the
hamlet of Bagnoli. Follow the enclosing
ridge to the left, to where its slope cuts
athwart plain and sea and sky; there close
upon the coast lies the island rock of Nisida,
meeting-place of Cicero and Brutus after
Cæsar's death. Turn to the opposite quarter of the plain. First rises the cliff of
Camaldoli, where from their oak-shadowed
lawn the monks look forth upon as fair
a prospect as is beheld by man. Lower
hills succeed, hiding Pozzuoli and the inner
curve of its bay; behind them, too, is the
nook which shelters Lake Avernus; and at
a little distance, by the further shore, are
the ruins of Cumæ, first home of the Greeks
upon Italian soil. A long promontory curves

round the gulf; the dark crag at the end
of it is Cape Misenum, and a little on the
hither side, obscured in remoteness, lies
what once was Baiæ. Behind the promontory gleams again a blue line of sea. The
low length of Procida is its limit, and behind
that, crowning the view, stands the moun-
tain-height of Ischia.

Over all, the hues of an autumn evening
in Campania. From behind a bulk of cloud,
here and there tossed by high wind currents
into fantastic shapes, sprang rays of fire,
burning to the zenith. Between the sea-
beach at Bagnoli and the summit of Ischia,
tract followed upon tract of colour that each
moment underwent a subtle change, dark-
ening here, there fading into exquisite trans-
parencies of distance, till by degrees the
islands lost projection and became mere
films against the declining day. The plain
was ruddy with dead vine-leaves, and golden
with the decaying foliage of the poplars;
Camaldoli and its neighbour heights stood
gorgeously enrobed. In itself, a picture so

beautiful that the eye wearied with delight ; in its memories, a source of solemn joy, inexhaustible for ever.

"I suppose," said Mallard, in the undertone of reflection, "the pagan associations of Naples are a great obstacle to Mrs. Baske's enjoyment of the scenery."

"She admits that."

"By-the-bye, what are likely to be the relations between her and Miss Doran ?"

"I have wondered. They seem to keep on terms of easy correspondence. But doesn't Cecily herself throw any light on that point ?"

Mallard made a pause before answering.

"You must remember that I know very little of her. I have never spoken more intimately with her than you yourself have. Naturally, since she has ceased to be a child, I have kept my distance. In fact, I shall be heartily glad when the next three years are over, and we can shake hands with a definite good-bye."

"What irritates you ?" inquired Spence,

with a smile which recognized a phase of his friend's character.

"The fact of my position. A nice thing for a fellow like me to have charge of a fortune! It oppresses me—the sense of responsibility; I want to get the weight off my shoulders. What the deuce did her father mean by burdening me in this way?"

"He foresaw nothing of the kind," said Spence, amused. "Only the unlikely event of Trench's death left you sole trustee. If Doran purposed anything at all—why, who knows what it may have been?"

Mallard refused to meet the other's look; his eyes were fixed on the horizon.

"All the same, the event was possible, and he should have chosen another man of business. It's worse than being rich on my own account. I have dreams of a national repudiation of debt; I imagine dock-companies failing and banks stopping payment. It disturbs my work; I am tired of it. Why can't I transfer the affair to some trustworthy and competent person; your-

self, for instance ? Why didn't Doran select
you, to begin with—the natural man to
associate with Trench ?"

"Who never opened a book save his
ledger; who was the model of a reputable
dealer in calicoes ; who—— "

"I apologize," growled Mallard.   "But
you know in what sense I spoke."

"Pray, what has Cecily become since I
saw her in London ? " asked the other, after
a pause, during which he smiled his own
interpretation of Mallard's humour.

"A very superior young person, I assure
you," was the reply, gravely spoken.   "Miss
Doran is a young woman of her time ; she
ranks with the emancipated ; she is as far
above the Girton girl as that interesting
creature is above the product of an establishment for young ladies.   Miss Doran has no
prejudices, and, in the vulgar sense of the
word, no principles.   She is familiar with
the Latin classics and with the Parisian
feuilletons ; she knows all about the newest
religion, and can tell you Sarcey's opinion

of the newest play. Miss Doran will discuss with you the merits of Sarah Bernhardt
in 'La Dame aux Camélias,' or the literary
theories of the brothers Goncourt. I am
not sure that she knows much about Shake-
speare, but her appreciation of Baudelaire is
exquisite. I don't think she is naturally
very cruel, but she can plead convincingly
the cause of vivisection. Miss Doran——"

Spence interrupted him with a burst of
laughter.

"All which, my dear fellow, simply
means that you—— "

Mallard, in his turn, interrupted gruffly.

"Precisely: that I am the wrong man to
hold even the position of steward to one
so advanced. What have I to do with
heiresses and fashionable ladies? I have
my work to get on with, and it shall not
suffer from the intrusion of idlers."

"I see you direct your diatribe half
against Mrs. Lessingham. How has she
annoyed you?"

"Annoyed me? You never were more

mistaken. It's with myself that I am annoyed."

" On what account ? "

" For being so absurd as to question sometimes whether my responsibility doesn't extend beyond stock and share. I ask myself whether Doran—who so befriended me, and put such trust in me, and paid me so well in advance for the duties I was to undertake—didn't take it for granted that I should exercise some influence in the matter of his daughter's education ? Is she growing up what he would have wished her to be ? And if—— "

" Why, it's no easy thing to say what views he had on this subject. The lax man, we know, is often enough severe with his own womankind. But as you have given me no description of what Cecily really is, I can offer no judgment. Wait till I have seen her. Doubtless she fulfils her promise of being beautiful ? "

" Yes ; there is no denying her beauty."

" As for her *modernité*, why, Mr. Ross

Mallard is a singular person to take exception on that score."

"I don't know about that. When did I ever say that the modern woman was my ideal ?"

"When had you ever a good word for the system which makes of woman a dummy and a kill-joy ?"

"That has nothing to do with the question," replied Mallard, preserving a tone of gruff impartiality. "Have I been faithful to my stewardship ? When I consented to Cecily's—to Miss Doran's passing from Mrs. Elgar's care to that of Mrs. Lessingham, was I doing right ?"

"Mallard, you are a curious instance of the puritan conscience surviving in a man whose intellect is liberated. The note of your character, including your artistic character, is this conscientiousness. Without it, you would have had worldly success long ago. Without it, you wouldn't talk nonsense of Cecily Doran. Had you rather she were co-operating with Mrs. Baske in a scheme to rebuild all the chapels in Lancashire ?"

"There is a medium."

"Why, yes. A neither this nor that, an insipid refinement, a taste for culture moderated by reverence for Mrs. Grundy."

"Perhaps you are right. It's only occasionally that I am troubled in this way. But I heartily wish the three years remaining were over."

"And the 'definite good-bye' spoken. A good phrase, that of yours. What possessed you to come here just now, if it disturbs you to be kept in mind of these responsibilities ?"

"I should find it hard to tell you. The very sense of responsibility, I suppose. But, as I said, I am not going to stay in Naples."

"You'll come and give us a 'definite good-bye' before you leave ?"

Mallard said nothing, but turned and began to move on. They passed one of the sentry-boxes which here along the ridge

mark the limits of Neapolitan excise; a
boy-soldier, musket in hand, cast curious
glances at them. After walking in silence
for a few minutes, they began to descend
the eastern face of the hill, and before them
lay that portion of the great gulf which
pictures have made so familiar. The landscape
was still visible in all its main details, still
softly suffused with warm colours from the
west. About the cone of Vesuvius a darkly
purple cloud was gathering; the twin height
of Somma stood clear and of a rich brown.
Naples, the many-coloured, was seen in
profile, climbing from the Castel dell' Ovo,
around which the sea slept, to the rock of
Sant' Elmo; along the curve of the Chiaia
lights had begun to glimmer. Far withdrawn, the craggy promontory of Sorrento
darkened to profoundest blue; and Capri
veiled itself in mist.

CHAPTER II.

CECILY DORAN.

VILLA SANNAZARO had no architectural beauty; it was a building of considerable size, irregular, in need of external repair. Through the middle of it ran a great arch-way, guarded by copies of the two Molossian hounds which stand before the Hall of Animals in the Vatican; beneath the arch, on the right-hand side, was the main entrance to the house. If you passed straight through, you came out upon a terrace, where grew a magnificent stone-pine and some robust agaves. The view hence was uninterrupted, embracing the line of the bay from Posilipo to Cape Minerva. From the parapet bordering the platform you looked over a descent of twenty feet, into a downward-sloping vineyard.

Formerly the residence of an old Neapolitan family, the villa had gone the way of many such ancestral abodes, and was now let out among several tenants.

The Spences were established here for the winter. On the occasion of his marriage, three years ago, Edward Spence relinquished his connection with a shipping firm, which he represented in Manchester, and went to live in London; a year and a half later he took his wife to Italy, where they had since remained. He was not wealthy, but had means sufficient to his demands and prospects. Thinking for himself in most matters, he chose to abandon money-making at the juncture when most men deem it incumbent upon them to press their efforts in that direction; business was repugnant to him, and he saw no reason why he should sacrifice his own existence to put a possible family in more than easy circumstances. He had the inclinations of a student, but was untroubled by any desire to distinguish himself; freedom from the demands of the office meant to him the possibility of living where he chose, and devoting to his books the best part of the day instead of its fragmentary leisure. His choice in marriage was most happy. Eleanor Spence had passed her maiden life in Manchester, but with parents of healthy mind and of more literature than generally falls to the lot of a commercial family. Pursuing a natural development, she allied herself with her husband's freedom of intellect, and found her nature's opportunities in the life which was to him most suitable. By a rare chance, she was the broader-minded of the two, the more truly impartial. Her emancipation from dogma had been so gradual, so unconfused by external pressure, that from her present standpoint she could look back with calmness and justice on all the stages she had left behind. With her cousin Miriam she could sympathize in a way impossible to Spence, who, by-the-bye, somewhat misrepresented his wife in the account he gave to Mallard of their Sunday experiences.

Puritanism was familiar to her by more than speculation ; in the compassion with which she regarded Miriam there was no mixture of contempt, as in her husband's case. On the other hand, she did not pretend to read completely her cousin's heart and mind ; she knew that there was no simple key to Miriam's character, and the quiet study of its phases from day to day deeply interested her.

Cecily Doran had been known to Spence from childhood ; her father was his intimate friend. But Eleanor had only made the girl's acquaintance in London, just after her marriage, when Cecily was spending a season there with her aunt, Mrs. Lessingham. Mallard's ward was then little more than fifteen ; after several years of weak health, she had entered upon a vigorous maidenhood, and gave such promise of free, joyous, aspiring life as could not but strongly affect the sympathies of a woman like Eleanor. Three years prior to that, at the time of her father's death, Cecily was living with

Mrs. Elgar, a widow, and her daughter
Miriam, the latter on the point of marrying
(at eighteen) one Mr. Baske, a pietistic
mill-owner, aged fifty. It then seemed
very doubtful whether Cecily would live
to mature years ; she had been motherless
from the age of two, and the difficulty
with those who brought her up was to re-
press an activity of mind which seemed to
be one cause of her bodily feebleness. In
those days there was certainly a strong
affection between her and Miriam, and it
showed no sign of diminution in either
when, on Mrs. Elgar's death, a year and a
half after Miriam's marriage, Cicely passed
into the care of her father's sister, a lady of
moderate fortune, of parts and attainments,
and with a great love of cosmopolitan life.
A few months more and Mrs. Baske was
to be a widow, childless, left in possession
of some eight hundred a year, her house at
Bartles, and a local importance which she
prized so much as to determine on living
as hitherto. With the exception of her

brother, away in London, she had no near
kin. It would now have been a great solace
to her if Cecily Doran could have been her
companion; but the young girl was in
Paris, or Berlin, or St. Petersburg, and, as
Miriam was soon to learn, the material distance between them meant little in comparison with the spiritual remoteness which
resulted from Cecily's education under Mrs.
Lessingham. They corresponded, however,
and at first frequently; but letters gradually
grew shorter on both sides, and arrived less
often. When news of Miriam's illness
reached Paris, it was some months since
Cecily had written; instantly she repaired
her omissions, and was constant in inquiry
thenceforth. The two were now to meet
for the first time since Cecily was a child of
fourteen.

The ladies arrived at the villa about
eleven o'clock. Miriam had shown herself
indisposed to speak of them, both last
evening, when Mallard was present, and
again this morning when alone with her

relatives ; at breakfast she was even more taciturn than usual, and kept her room for an hour after the meal. Then, however, she came to sit with Eleanor, and remained so as to be present when the visitors were announced.

Mrs. Lessingham did not answer to the common idea of a strong-minded woman. At forty-seven she preserved much natural grace of bearing, a good complexion, pleasantly mobile features. Her dress was in excellent taste, tending to elaboration, such as becomes a lady who makes some figure in the world of ease. Little wrinkles at the outer corners of her eyes assisted her look of placid thoughtfulness; when she spoke, these were wont to disappear, and the expression of her face became an animated intelligence, an eager curiosity, or a vivacious good-humour. Her lips gave a hint of sarcasm, but this was reserved for special occasions; as a rule her habit of speech was suave, much observant of amenities. One might have imagined that she had enjoyed a calm life, but this was far from being the case. The daughter of a country solicitor, she married early—for love, and the issue was disastrous. Above her right temple, just at the roots of the hair, a scar was discoverable ; it was the memento of an occasion on which her husband aimed a blow at her with a mantelpiece ornament, and came within an ace of murder. Intimates of the household said that the aggravation was great—that Mrs. Lessingham's gift of sarcasm had that morning displayed itself much too brilliantly. Still, the missile was an extreme retort, and on the whole it could not be wondered at that husband and wife resolved to live apart in future. Mr. Lessingham was, in fact, an aristocratic boor, and his wife never puzzled so much over any intellectual difficulty as she did over the question how, as a girl, she came to imagine herself enamoured of him. She was not, I believe, singular in her concernment with such a personal problem.

" It is six years since I was in Italy," she
said, when greetings were over, and she had
seated herself. " Don't you envy me my
companion, Mrs. Spence? If anything could
revive one's first enjoyment, it would be the
sight of Cecily's."

Cecily was sitting by Miriam, whose hand
she had only just relinquished. Her anxious
and affectionate inquiries moved Miriam to
a smile which seemed rather of indulgence
than warm kindness.

" How little we thought where our next
meeting would be !" Cecily was saying,
when the eyes of the others turned upon
her at her aunt's remark.

Noble beauty can scarcely be dissociated
from harmony of utterance ; voice and
visage are the correspondent means whereby
spirit addresses itself to the ear and eye.
Had you heard Cecily Doran speaking where
you could not see her, you must have
turned in that direction, have listened
eagerly for the sounds to repeat themselves,
and then have moved forward to discover

the speaker. That, as you are aware, is by
no means necessarily the case where persons
are concerned who have a "good voice;"
the divinest singer may leave you unaffected
by the tone of her speech. Cecily could not
sing, but her voice declared her of those
who think in song, whose minds are modu-
lated to the poetry, not to the prose, of life.

Her enunciation had the peculiar finish
which is acquired in intercourse with the
best cosmopolitan society, the best in a
worthy sense. Four years ago, when she
left Lancashire, she had a touch of provincial
accent,—Miriam, though she spoke well, was
not wholly free from it,—but now it was
impossible to discover by listening to her
from what part of England she came. Mrs.
Lessingham, whose admirable tact and
adaptability rendered her unimpeachable in
such details, had devoted herself with artistic
zeal to her niece's training for the world;
the pupil's natural aptitude ensured perfec-
tion in the result. Cecily's manner accorded
with her tone of speech; it had every

charm derivable from youth, yet nothing of immaturity. She was as completely at her ease as Mrs. Lessingham, and as much more graceful in her self-control as the advantages of nature made inevitable.

Miriam looked very cold, very severe, very English, by the side of this brilliant girl. The thinness and pallor of her features became more noticeable; the provincial faults of her dress were painfully obvious. Cecily was not robust, but her form lacked no development appropriate to her years, and its beauty was displayed by Parisian handiwork. In this respect, too, she had changed remarkably since Miriam last saw her, when she was such a frail child. Her hair of dark gold showed itself beneath a hat which Eleanor Spence kept regarding with frank admiration, so novel it was in style, and so perfectly suitable to its wearer. Her gloves, her shoes, were no less perfect; from head to foot nothing was to be found that did not become her, that was not faultless in its kind.

At the same time, nothing that suggested idle expense or vanity. To dwell at all upon the subject would be a disproportion, but for the note of contrast that was struck. In an assembly of well-dressed people, no one would have remarked Cecily's attire, unless to praise its quiet distinction. In the Spences' sitting-room it became another matter; it gave emphasis to differences of character; it distinguished the atmosphere of Cecily's life from that breathed by her old friends.

"We are going to read together Goethe's 'Italienische Reise,'" continued Mrs. Lessingham. "It was of quite infinite value to me when I first was here. In each town I *tuned* my thoughts by it, to use a phrase which sounds like affectation, but has a very real significance."

"It was much the same with me," observed Spence.

"Yes, but you had the inestimable advantage of knowing the classics. And Cecily, I am thankful to say, at least has something of Latin; an ode of Horace, which I look at with fretfulness, yields her its meaning. Last night, when I was tired and willing to be flattered, she tried to make me believe it was **not** yet too late to learn."

"Surely not," said Eleanor, gracefully.

"But Goethe—you remember he says that the desire to see Italy had become an illness with him. I know so well what that means. Cecily will never know; the happiness has come before longing for it had ceased to be a pleasure."

It was not so much affection as pride that her voice expressed when she referred to her niece; the same in her look, which was less tender than gratified and admiring. Cecily smiled in return, but was not wholly attentive; her eyes constantly turned to Miriam, endeavouring, though vainly, to exchange a glance.

Mrs. Lessingham was well aware of the difficulty of addressing to Mrs. Baske any remark on natural topics which could engage her sympathy, yet to ignore her presence was impossible.

"Do you think of seeing Rome and the northern cities when your health is established?" she inquired, in a voice which skilfully avoided any presumption of the reply. "Or shall you return by sea?"

"I am not a very good sailor," answered Miriam, with sufficient suavity, "and I shall probably go back by land. But I don't think I shall stop anywhere."

"It will be wiser, no doubt," said Mrs. Lessingham, "to leave the rest of Italy for another visit. To see Naples first, and then go north, is very much like taking dessert before one's substantial dinner. I'm a little sorry that Cecily begins here; but it was better to come and enjoy Naples with her friends this winter. I hope we shall spend most of our time in Italy for a year or two."

Conversation took its natural course, and presently turned to the subject—inexhaustible at Naples—of the relative advantages of this and that situation for an abode. Mrs. Lessingham, turning to the window, expressed her admiration of the view it afforded.

"I think it is still better from Mrs. Baske's sitting-room," said Eleanor, who had been watching Cecily, and thought that she might be glad of an opportunity of private talk with Miriam. And Cecily at once availed herself of the suggestion.

"Would you let me see it, Miriam?" she asked. "If it is not troublesome——"

Miriam rose, and they went out together. In silence they passed along the corridor, and when they had entered her room Miriam walked at once to the window. Then she half turned, and her eyes fell before Cecily's earnest gaze.

"I did so wish to be with you in your illness!" said the girl, with affectionate warmth. "Indeed, I would have come if I could have been of any use. After all the trouble you used to have with my wretched headaches and ailments——"

"You never have anything of the kind now," said Miriam, with her indulgent smile.

"Never. I am in what Mr. Mallard calls aggressive health. But it shocks me to see how pale you still are, Miriam. I thought the voyage and these ten days at Naples—— And you have such a careworn look. Cannot you throw off your troubles under this sky?"

"You know that the sky matters very little to me, Cecily."

"If I could give you only half my delight! I was awake before dawn this morning, and it was impossible to lie still. I dressed and stood at the open window. I couldn't see the sun itself as it rose, but I watched the first beams strike on Capri and the sea; and I tried to make a drawing of the island as it then looked,—a poor little daub, but it will be precious in bringing back to my mind all I felt when I was busy with it. Such feeling I have never known; as if every nerve in me had received an exquisite new sense. I keep saying to myself, ' Is this really Naples ?' Let us go on to the balcony. Oh, you *must* be glad with me ! "

Freed from the constraint of formal colloquy, and overcoming the slight embarrassment caused by what she knew of Miriam's thoughts, Cecily revealed her nature as it lay beneath the graces with which education had endowed her. This enthusiasm was no new discovery to Miriam, but in the early days it had attached itself to far other things. Cecily seemed to have forgotten that she was ever in sympathy with the mood which imposed silence on her friend. Her eyes drank light from the landscape; her beauty was transfigured by passionate reception of all the influences this scene could exercise upon heart and mind. She leaned on the railing of the balcony, and gazed until tears of ecstasy made her sight dim.

" Let us see much of each other whilst we are here," she said suddenly, turning to Miriam. " I could never have dreamt of our being together in Italy; it is a happy fate, and gives me all kinds of hope. We will be often alone together in glorious places. We will talk it over; that is better than writing. You shall understand me, Miriam. You shall get as well and strong as I am, and know what I mean when I speak of the joy of living. We shall be sisters again, like we used to be."

Miriam smiled and shook her head.

"Tell me about things at home. Is Miss Baske well?"

"Quite well. I have had two letters from her since I was here. She wished me to give you her love."

"I will write to her. And is old Don still alive?"

"Yes; but very feeble, poor old fellow. He forgets even to be angry with the baker's boy."

Cecily laughed with a moved playfulness.

"He has forgotten me. I don't like to be forgotten by any one who ever cared for me."

There was a pause. They came back into the room, and Cecily, with a look of hesitation, asked quietly :

"Have you heard of late from Reuben ?"

Miriam, with averted eyes, answered simply, "No." Again there was silence, until Cecily, moving about the room, came to the "St. Cecilia."

"So my patron saint is always before you. I am glad of that. Where is the original of this picture, Miriam ? I forget."

"I never knew."

"Oh, I wished to speak to you of Mr. Mallard. You met him yesterday. Had you much conversation ?"

"A good deal. He dined with us."

"Did he ? I thought it possible. And do you like him ?"

"I couldn't say until I knew him better."

"It isn't easy to know him, I think," said Cecily, in a reflective and perfectly natural tone, smiling thoughtfully. "But he is a very interesting man, and I wish he would be more friendly with me. I tried

hard to win his confidence on the journey
from Genoa, but I didn't seem to have much
success. I fancy "—she laughed—" that he
is still in the habit of regarding me as a
little girl, who wouldn't quite understand
him if he spoke of serious things. When
I wished to speak of his painting, he would
only joke. That annoyed me a little, and
I tried to let him see that it did, with the
result that he refused to speak of anything
for a long time."

"What does Mr. Mallard paint?" Miriam
asked, half absently.

"Landscape," was the reply, given with
veiled surprise. "Did you never see anything of his?"

"I remember, the Bradshaws have a
picture by him in their dining-room. They
showed it me when I was last in Manchester.
I'm afraid I looked at it very inattentively,
for it has never re-entered my mind from
that day to this. But I was ill at the time."

"His pictures are neglected," said Cecily,
"but people who understand them say they

have great value. If he has anything accepted by the Academy, it is sure to be hung out of sight. I think he is wrong to exhibit there at all. Academies are foolish things, and always give most encouragement to the men who are worth least. When there is talk of such subjects, I never lose an opportunity of mentioning Mr. Mallard's name, and telling all I can about his work. Some day I shall, perhaps, be able to help him. I will insist on every friend of mine who buys pictures at all possessing at least one of Mr. Mallard's; then, perhaps, he will condescend to talk with me of serious things."

She added the last sentence merrily, meeting Miriam's look with the frankest eyes.

"Does Mrs. Lessingham hold the same opinion?" Miriam inquired.

"Oh yes! Aunt, of course, knows far more about art than I do, and she thinks very highly indeed of Mr. Mallard. Not long ago she met M. Lambert at a friend's house in Paris—the French critic who has just been writing about English landscape—

and he mentioned Mr. Mallard with great respect. That was splendid, wasn't it?"

She spoke with joyous spiritedness. However modern, Cecily, it was clear, had caught nothing of the disease of pococurantism. Into whatever pleased her or enlisted her sympathies, she threw all the glad energies of her being. The scornful remark on the Royal Academy was, one could see, not so much a mere echo of advanced opinion, as a piece of championship in a friend's cause. The respect with which she mentioned the name of the French critic, her exultation in his dictum, were notes of a youthful idealism which interpreted the world nobly, and took its stand on generous beliefs.

"Mr. Mallard will help you to see Naples, no doubt," said Miriam.

"Indeed, I wish he would. But he distinctly told us that he has no time. He is going to Amalfi in a few days, to work. I begged him at least to go to Pompeii with us, but he frowned—as he so often does—and seemed unwilling to be persuaded; so I said no more. There again, I feel sure he was afraid of being annoyed by trifling talk in such places. But one mustn't judge an artist like other men. To be sure, anything I could say or think would be trivial compared with what is in *his* mind."

" But isn't it rather discourteous?" Miriam observed impartially.

" Oh, I could never think of it in that way! An artist is privileged; he must defend his time and his sensibilities. The common terms of society have no application to him. Don't you feel that, Miriam?"

" I know so little of art and artists. But such a claim seems to me very strange."

Cecily laughed.

" This is one of a thousand things we will talk about. Art is the grandest thing in the world; it means everything that is strong and beautiful — statues, pictures, poetry, music. How could one live without art? The artist is born a prince among men. What has he to do with the rules by which common people must direct their lives? Before long, you will feel this as deeply as I do, Miriam. We are in Italy, Italy!"

"Shall we go back to the others?" Miriam suggested, in a voice which contrasted curiously with that exultant utterance.

"Yes; it is time."

Cecily's eyes fell on the plans of the chapel, which were still lying open.

"What is this?" she asked. "Something in Naples? Oh no!"

"It's nothing," said Miriam, carelessly. "Come, Cecily."

The visitors took their leave just as the midday cannon boomed from Sant' Elmo. They had promised to come and dine in a day or two. After their departure, Miriam showed as little disposition to make comments as she had to indulge in expectation before their arrival. Eleanor and her husband put less restraint upon themselves.

"Heavens!" cried Spence, when they were alone; "what astounding capacity of growth was in that child!"

"She is a swift and beautiful creature!" said Eleanor, in a warm undertone characteristic of her when she expressed admiration.

"I wish I could have overheard the interview in Miriam's room."

"I never felt more curiosity about anything. Pity one is not a psychological artist. I should have stolen to the keyhole and committed eavesdropping with a glow of self-approval."

"I half understand our friend Mallard."

"So do I, Ned."

They looked at each other and smiled significantly.

That evening Spence again had a walk with the artist. He returned to the villa alone, and only just in time to dress for dinner. Guests were expected, Mr. and Mrs. Bradshaw of Manchester, old acquaintances of the Spences and of Miriam. When it had become known that Mrs. Baske, advised to pass the winter in a mild climate, was about to accept an invitation from her cousin and go by sea to Naples, the Bradshaws, to the astonishment of all their friends, offered to accompany her. It was the first time that either of them had left England, and they seemed most unlikely people to be suddenly affected with a zeal for foreign travel. Miriam gladly welcomed their proposal, and it was put into execution.

When Spence entered the room, his friends had already arrived. Mr. Bradshaw stood in the attitude familiar to him when on his own hearthrug, his back turned to that part of the wall where in England would have been a fireplace, and one hand thrust into the pocket of his evening coat.

"I tell you what it is, Spence!" he exclaimed. "I'm very much afraid I shall be committing an assault. Certainly I shall if I don't soon learn some good racy Italian. I must make out a little list of sentences, and get you or Mrs. Spence to translate them. Such as 'Do you take me for a fool?' or 'Be off, you scoundrel!' or 'I'll break every bone in your body!' That's the kind of thing practically needed in Naples, I find."

"Been in conflict with coachmen again?" asked Spence, laughing.

"Slightly! Never got into such a help-less rage in my life. Two fellows kept up with me this afternoon for a couple of miles or so. Now, what makes me so mad is the assumption of these blackguards that I don't know my own mind. I go out for a stroll, and the first cabby I pass wants to take me to Pozzuoli or Vesuvius—or Jericho, for aught I know. It's no use showing him that I haven't the slightest intention of going to any such place. What the deuce! Does the fellow suppose he can persuade me or badger me into doing what I've no mind to do? Does he take me for an ass? It's the insult of the thing that riles me! The same if I look in at a shop-window; out rushes a gabbling swindler, and wants to drag me in—— "

"Only to *take* you in, Mr. Bradshaw," interjected Eleanor.

" Good ! To take me in, with a vengeance.
Why, if I've a mind to buy, shan't I go in
of my own accord ?   And isn't it a sure and
certain thing that I shall never spend a
halfpenny with a scoundrel who attacks me
like that ? "

" How can you expect foreigners to reason,
Jacob ? " exclaimed Mrs. Bradshaw.

" You should take these things as compli-
ments," remarked Spence.   " They see an
Englishman coming along, and as a matter
of course they consider him a person of
wealth and leisure, who will be grateful to
any one for suggesting how he can kill time.
Having nothing in the world to do but
enjoy himself, why shouldn't the English
lord drive to Baiæ and back, just to get an
appetite ? "

" Lord, eh ? " growled Mr. Bradshaw,
rising on his toes, and smiling with a certain
satisfaction.

Threescore years all but two sat lightly
on Jacob Bush Bradshaw. His cheek was
ruddy, his eyes had the lustre of health ; in

the wrinkled forehead you saw activity of brain, and on his lips the stubborn independence of a Lancashire employer of labour. Prosperity had set its mark upon him, that peculiarly English prosperity which is so intimately associated with spotless linen, with a good cut of clothes, with scant but valuable jewellery, with the absence of any perfume save that which suggests the morning tub. He was a manufacturer of silk. The provincial accent notwithstanding, his conversation on general subjects soon declared him a man of logical mind and of much homely information. A sufficient self-esteem allied itself with his force of character, but robust amiability prevented this from becoming offensive; he had the sense of humour, and enjoyed a laugh at himself as well as at other people. Though his life had been absorbed in the pursuit of solid gain, he was no scorner of the attainments which lay beyond his own scope, and in these latter years, now that the fierce struggle was decided in his favour, he often gave proof of a liberal curiosity. With regard to art and learning, he had the intelligence to be aware of his own defects; where he did not enjoy, he at least knew that he ought to have done so, and he had a suspicion that herein also progress could be made by stubborn effort, as in the material world. Finding himself abroad, he had set himself to observe and learn, with results now and then not a little amusing. The consciousness of wealth disposed him to intellectual generosity; standing on so firm a pedestal, he did not mind admitting that others might have a wider outlook. Italy was a poor country; personally and patriotically he had a pleasure in recognizing the fact, and this made it easier for him to concede the points of superiority which he heard attributed to her. Jacob was rigidly sincere; he had no touch of the snobbery which shows itself in sham admiration. If he liked a thing he said so, and strongly; if he felt no liking where his guide-book directed him to be enthusiastic, he kept silence and cudgelled his brains.

Equally ingenuous was his wife, but with results that argued a poorer nature. Mrs. Bradshaw had the heartiest and frankest contempt for all things foreign; in Italy she deemed herself among a people so inferior to the English that even to discuss the relative merits of the two nations would have been ludicrous. Life " abroad " she could not take as a serious thing; it amused or disgusted her, as the case might be—never occasioned her a grave thought. The proposal of this excursion, when first made to her, she received with mockery; when she saw that her husband meant something more than a joke, she took time to consider, and at length accepted the notion as a freak which possibly would be entertaining, and might at all events be indulged after a lifetime of sobriety. Entertainment she found in abundance. Though natural beauty made little if any appeal to her, she interested herself greatly in Vesuvius, regarding it as a serio-comic phenomenon which could only exist in a country inhabited by childish triflers.

Her memory was storing all manner of Italian absurdities—everything being an absurdity which differed from English habit and custom—to furnish her with matter for mirthful talk when she got safely back to Manchester and civilization. With respect to the things which Jacob was constraining himself to study — antiquities, sculptures, paintings, stored in the Naples museum—her attitude was one of jocose indifference or of half-tolerant contempt. Puritanism diluted with worldliness and a measure of common sense directed her views of art in general. Works such as the Farnese Hercules and the group about the Bull she looked upon much as she regarded the wall-scribbling of some dirty-minded urchin ; the robust matron is not horrified by such indecencies, but to be sure will not stand and examine them. "Oh, come along, Jacob !" she exclaimed to her husband, when, at their first visit to the Museum, he went to work at the antiques with his Murray. " I've no patience ! you ought to be ashamed of yourself!" Whether or not this was an advance upon the stern intolerance which made Miriam Baske refuse even to enter the building, I leave to your speculation.

The Bradshaws, as you have incidentally learnt, were staying at the *pension* selected by Mrs. Lessingham. Naturally the conversation at dinner turned much on that lady and her niece. With Cecily's father Mr. Bradshaw had been well acquainted, but Cecily herself he had not seen since her childhood, and his astonishment at meeting her as Miss Doran was great.

"What kind of society do they live among?" he asked of Spence. "Tip-top people, I suppose?"

"Not exactly what we understand by tip-top in England. Mrs. Lessingham's family connections are aristocratic, but she prefers the society of authors, artists—that kind of thing."

"Queer people for a young girl to make friends of, eh?"

"Well, there's Mallard, for instance.

" Ah, Mallard, to be sure."

Mrs. Bradshaw looked at her hostess and smiled knowingly.

" Miss Doran is rather fond of talking about Mr. Mallard," she remarked. " Did you notice that, Miriam ?"

" Yes, I did."

Jacob broke the silence.

" How does he get on with his painting ?" he asked—and it sounded very much as though the reference were to a man busy on the front door.

" He's never likely to be very popular," replied Spence, who of course had to adapt his remarks to the level of his guests' understanding. " There was something of his in this year's Academy, and it sold at a tolerable price."

" That thing of his that I bought, you remember—I find people don't see much in it. They complain that the colour's so dull. But then, as I always say, what else could you expect on a bit of Yorkshire moor in winter ? Is he going to paint anything here? Now, if he'd do me a bit of the bay, with Vesuvius smoking."

"That would be something like!" assented Mrs. Bradshaw.

When the ladies had left the dining-room, Mr. Bradshaw, over his cigarette, reverted to the subject of Cecily.

"I suppose the lass has had a first-rate education?"

"Of the very newest fashion for girls. I am told she reads Latin."

"By Jove!" cried the other, with sudden animation. "That reminds me of something I wanted to talk about. When I was leaving Manchester, I got together a few books, you know, that were likely to be useful over here. My friend Lomas, the bookseller, suggested them. 'Got a classical dictionary?' says he. 'Not I!' As you know, my schooling never went much beyond the three R's, and hanged if I knew what a classical dictionary was. 'Better take one,' says Lomas. 'You'll want to look up your gods and goddesses.'

So I took it, and I've been looking into it these last few days."

" Well ?"

Jacob had a comical look of perplexity and indignation. He thumped the table.

" Do you mean to tell me that's the kind of stuff boys are set to learn at school ? "

" A good deal of it comes in."

" Then all I can say is, no wonder the colleges turn out such a lot of young blackguards. Why, man, I could scarcely believe my eyes ! You mean to say that, if I'd had a son, he'd have been brought up on that kind of literature, and without me knowing anything about it ? Why, I've locked the book up ; I was ashamed to let it lay on the table."

" It's the old Lemprière, I suppose," said Spence, vastly amused. " The new dictionaries are toned down a good deal ; they weren't so squeamish in the old days."

" But the lads still read the books these things come out of, eh ? "

" Oh yes. It has always been one of

the most laughable inconsistencies in English morality. Anything you could find
in the dictionary is milk for babes compared with several Greek plays that have
to be read for examinations."

"It fair caps me, Spence! Classical
education that is, eh? That's what parsons
are bred on? And, by the Lord, you say
they're beginning it with girls?"

"Very zealously."

"Nay——!"

Jacob threw up his arms, and abandoned
the effort to express himself.

Later, when the guests were gone, this
recurred to Spence's mind, and, to Eleanor's
surprise, he broke into uproarious laughter.

"One of the best jokes I ever heard!
A fresh, first-hand judgment on the morality of the Classics by a plain-minded
English man of business." He told the
story. "And Bradshaw's perfectly right;
that's the best of it."

CHAPTER III.

THE BOARDING-HOUSE ON THE MERGELLINA.

I AM writing of the year 1878. Had you in that year consulted Baedeker, with a view to finding a genteel but not oppressively aristocratic *pension* in the open parts of Naples, your eye would have been directed by an asterisk to the establishment kept by Madame Glück on the Mergellina; a note advised you that it was frequented by English and Germans, and was very comfortable. The recommendation was a just one. Madame Glück enjoyed the advantage of having lived as many years in England as she had in Germany; her predilections leaned, if anything, to the English side, and the arrival of a "nice" English family always put her in excellent spirits. She then exhibited herself as an

Anglicized matron, perfectly familiar with
all the requirements, great and little, of
her guests, and, when minutiæ were once
settled, capable of meeting ladies and
gentlemen on terms of equality in her
drawing-room or at her table, where she
always presided. Indeed, there was much
true refinement in Madame Glück. You
had not been long in her house before she
found an opportunity of letting you know
that she prided herself on connection with
the family of the great musician, and, were
you a musician yourself, she would make
things very pleasant for you indeed : under
her roof there was nearly always some one
who played or sang well. It was her
desire that all who sat at her dinner-table—
the English people, at all events—should be
in evening-dress. She herself had no little
art in adorning herself so as to appear, what
she was, a lady, and yet not to conflict with
the ladies whose presence honoured her.

In the drawing-room, a few days after
the arrival of Mrs. Lessingham and her

niece, several members of the household were assembled in readiness for the second dinner-bell. There was Frau Wohlgemuth, a middle-aged lady with severe brows, utilizing spare moments over a German work on Greek sculpture. Certain plates in the book had before now caught the eye of Mrs. Bradshaw, and she in consequence regarded this innocent student as a person of most doubtful character, who, if in ignorance admitted to a respectable board-ing-house, should certainly have been got rid of as soon as the nature of her reading had been discovered. Frau Wohlgemuth had once or twice been astonished at the severe look fixed upon her by the buxom English lady, but happily would never receive an explanation of this silent animus. Then there was Fraülein Kriel, who had unwillingly incurred even more of Mrs. Bradshaw's displeasure, in that she, an unmarried person, had actually looked over the volume together with its possessor, not so much as blushing when she found

herself observed by strangers. The remaining persons were an English family,
a mother and three daughters, their name
Denyer. These ladies were no less a source
of contemptuous astonishment to Mrs.
Bradshaw than the shameless Germans, for
reasons which will be manifest when I have
described the family.

Mrs. Denyer was florid, vivacious, and
of a certain size. She had seen much of
the world, and prided herself on cosmopo-
litanism; the one thing with which she
could not dispense was intellectual society.
This would be her second winter at Naples,
but she gave her acquaintances to understand that Italy was by no means the
country of her choice; she preferred the
northern latitudes, because there the intellectual atmosphere was more bracing.
But for her daughters' sake she abode here:
" You know, my girls *adore* Italy."

Of these young ladies, the two elder—
Barbara and Madeline were their seductive
names—had good looks. Barbara, perhaps

twenty-two years old, was rather colourless, somewhat too slim, altogether a trifle limp; but you would have judged her pretty, and have approved her taste in dress. Madeline, a couple of years younger, enjoyed a more healthy physique and a less common comeliness, but in attire she seemed to aim at Herrick's "fine distraction" and "sweet disorder," without being able to compass the corresponding "wild civility." Her colours were ill-matched, her ornaments awkwardly worn; even her hair sought more freedom than was consistent with grace. The youngest girl, Zillah, who was about nineteen, had been less kindly dealt with by nature; like Barbara, she was of very light complexion, and this accentuated her plainness. She aimed at no compensation in costume, unless one took it for such that her sober garments exhibited a perfect neatness and a complete inoffensiveness. Zillah's was a good face, in spite of its unattractive features; she had a peculiarly earnest look, a reflective manner, and much conscientiousness of speech.

Common to the three was a resolve to
be modern, advanced and emancipated, or
perish in the attempt. Every one who spoke
with them must understand that they were
no everyday young ladies, imbued with
notions and prejudices recognized as feminine,
frittering away their lives amid the follies of
the drawing-room and of the circulating
library. Culture was their pursuit, hetero-
doxy their pride. If indeed it were true,
as Mrs. Bradshaw somewhat acrimoniously
declared, that they were all desperately
bent on capturing husbands, then assuredly
the poor girls went about their enterprise
with singular lack of discretion.

Each had her *rôle*. Barbara's was to
pose as the adorer of Italy, the enthusiastic
glorifier of Italian unity. She spoke Italian
feebly, but, with English people, never lost
an opportunity of babbling its phrases.
Speak to her of Rome, and before long she
was sure to murmur rapturously, " Roma
capitale d'Italia ! "—the watch-word of anti-
papal victory. Of English writers she loved,

or affected to love, those only who had found inspiration south of the Alps. The proud mother would tell you a story of Barbara's going up to the wall of Casa Guidi and kissing it. In her view, the modern Italians could do no wrong; they were divinely regenerate. She praised their architecture.

Madeline—whom her sisters addressed affectionately as "Mad"—professed a wider intellectual scope; less given to the melting mood than Barbara, less naïve in her enthusiasms, she took for her province æsthetic criticism in its totality, and shone rather in censure than in laudation. French she read passably; German she had talked so much of studying that it was her belief she had acquired it; Greek and Latin were not indeed linguistically known to her—one must pick one's phrases in speaking of Madeline—but from modern essayists who wrote in the flamboyant style she had gathered so much knowledge of these literatures as to be able to discourse of them

with a very fluent inaccuracy. With all
schools of painting she was, of course, quite
familiar; the great masters—vulgarly so
known—interested her but moderately, and
to praise them was to subject yourself in her
eyes to a suspicion of philistinism. From
her preceptors in this sphere, she had learnt
certain names, old and new, which stood
for more exquisite virtues, and the frequent
mention of them with a happy vagueness
made her conversation very impressive to
the generality of people. The same in
music. It goes without saying that Madeline was an indifferentist in politics and on
social questions; at the introduction of such
topics, she smiled.

Zillah's position was one of more difficulty.
With nothing of her sisters' superficial
cleverness, with a mind that worked slowly,
and a memory irretentive, she had a
genuine desire to instruct herself, and that
in a solid way. She alone studied with real
persistence, and, by the irony of fate, she
alone continually exposed her ignorance,

committed gross blunders, was guilty of
deplorable lapses of memory. Her unhappy
lot kept her in a constant state of nervousness and shame. She had no worldly tact,
no command of her modest resources, yet
her zeal to support the credit of the family
was always driving her into hurried speech,
sure to end in some disastrous pitfall.
Conscious of æsthetic defects, Zillah had
chosen for her specialty the study of the
history of civilization. But for being a
Denyer, she might have been content to say
that she studied history, and in that case
her life might also have been solaced by the
companionship of readable books; but, as
modernism would have it, she could not be
content to base her historical inquiries on
anything less than strata of geology and
biological elements, with the result that she
toiled day by day at nasty little primers
and compendia, and only learnt one chapter
that it might be driven out of her head
by the next. Equally out of deference to
her sisters, she smothered her impulses to

conventional piety, and made believe that
her spiritual life supported itself on the
postulates of science. As a result of all
which, the poor girl was not very happy, but
in that again did she not give proof of
belonging to her time?

There existed a Mr. Denyer, but this
gentleman was very seldom indeed in the
bosom of his family. Letters—and remittances—came from him from the most sur-
prising quarters of the globe. His profession
was that of speculator at large, and, with
small encouragement of any kind, he toiled
unceasingly to support his wife and daughters
in their elegant leisure. At one time he
was eagerly engaged in a project for making
starch from potatoes in the south of Ireland.
When this failed, he utilized a knowledge of
Spanish—casually picked up, like all his
acquirements—and was next heard of at
Vera Cruz, where he dealt in cochineal,
indigo, sarsaparilla, and logwood. Yellow
fever interfered with his activity, and after
a brief sojourn with his family in the United

States, where they had joined him with the idea of making a definite settlement, he heard of something promising in Egypt, and thither repaired. A spare, vivacious, pathetically sanguine man, always speaking of the day when he would "settle down" in enjoyment of a moderate fortune, and most obviously doomed never to settle at all, save in the final home of mortality.

Mrs. Lessingham and her niece entered the room. On Cecily, as usual, all eyes were more or less openly directed. Her evening dress was simple—though with the simplicity not to be commanded by every one who wills—and her demeanour very far from exacting general homage; but her birthright of distinction could not be laid aside, and the suave Madame Glück was not singular in recognizing that here was such a guest as did not every day grace her *pension*. Barbara and Madeline Denyer never looked at her without secret pangs. In appearance, however, they were very friendly, and Cecily had met their overtures from the first with the simple goodwill natural to her. She went and seated herself by Madeline, who had on her lap a little portfolio.

"These are the drawings of which I spoke," said Madeline, half opening the portfolio.

"Mr. Marsh's ? Oh, I shall be glad to see them !"

"Of course, we ought to have daylight, but we'll look at them again to-morrow. You can form an idea of their character."

They were small water-colours, the work —as each declared in fantastic signature— of one Clifford Marsh, spoken of by the Denyers, and by Madeline in particular, as a personal friend. He was expected to arrive any day in Naples. The subjects, Cecily had been informed, were natural scenery ; the style, impressionist. Impressionism was no novel term to Cecily, and in Paris she had had her attention intelligently directed to good work in that kind ; she knew, of course, that, like every other style, it must be judged with reference to its success in achieving the end proposed. But the first glance at the first of Mr. Marsh's productions perplexed her. A study on the Roman Campagna, said Madeline. It might just as well, for all Cecily could determine, have been a study of cloud-forms, or of a storm at sea, or of anything, or of nothing; nor did there seem to be any cogent reason why it should be looked at one way up rather than the other. Was this genius, or impudence?

"You don't know the Campagna yet," remarked Madeline, finding that the other kept silence. "Of course, you can't appreciate the marvellous truthfulness of this impression; but it gives you new emotions, doesn't it?"

Mrs. Lessingham would have permitted herself to reply with a pointed affirmative. Cecily was too considerate of others' feelings for that, yet had not the habit of smooth falsehood.

"I am not very familiar with this kind of work," she said. "Please let me just look and think, and tell me your own thoughts about each."

Madeline was not displeased. Already she had discovered that in most directions Miss Doran altogether exceeded her own reach, and that it was not safe to talk conscious nonsense to her. The tone of modesty seemed unaffected, and, as Madeline had reasons for trying to believe in Clifford Marsh, it gratified her to feel that here at length she might tread firmly and hold her own. The examination of the drawings proceeded, with the result that Cecily's original misgiving was strongly confirmed. What would Ross Mallard say? Mallard's own work was not of the impressionist school, and he might suffer prejudice to direct him ; but she had a conviction of how his remarks would sound were this portfolio submitted to him. Genius—scarcely. And if not, then assuredly the other thing, and that in flagrant degree.

Most happily, the dinner-bell came with its peremptory interruption.

"I must see them again to-morrow," said Cecily, in her pleasantest voice.

At table, the ladies were in a majority. Mr. Bradshaw was the only man past middle life. Next in age to him came Mr. Mussel-white, who looked about forty, and whose aquiline nose, high forehead, light bushy whiskers, and air of vacant satisfaction, marked him as the aristocrat of the assembly. This gentleman suffered under a truly aristocratic affliction—the ever-reviving diffi-culty of passing his day. Mild in demeanour, easy in the discharge of petty social obliga-tions, perfectly inoffensive, he came and went like a vivified statue of gentlemanly *ennui*. Every morning there arrived for him a consignment of English newspapers; these were taken to his bedroom at nine o'clock, together with a cup of chocolate. They presumably occupied him until he appeared in the drawing-room, just before the hour of luncheon, when, in spite of the freshness of his morning attire, he seemed already burdened by the blank of time, always sitting down to the meal with an audible sigh of gratitude. Invariably he addressed to his neighbour a remark on the direction of the smoke from Vesuvius. If the neighbour happened to be uninformed in things Neapolitan, Mr. Musselwhite seized the occasion to explain at length the meteorologic significance of these varying fumes. Luncheon over, he rose like one who is summoned to a painful duty; in fact, the great task of the day was before him—the struggle with time until the hour of dinner. You would meet him sauntering sadly about the gardens of the Villa Nazionale, often looking at his watch, which he always regulated by the cannon of Sant' Elmo; or gazing with lack-lustre eye at a shop-window in the Via Roma; or sitting with a little glass of Marsala before him in one of the fashionable *cafés*, sunk in despondency. But when at length he appeared at the dinner-table, once more fresh from his toilet, then did a gleam of animation transform his countenance; for the victory

was won; yet again was old time defeated.
Then would he discourse his best. Two
topics had he: the weather, and "my
brother the baronet's place in Lincolnshire."
The manner of his monologue on this second
and more fruitful subject was really touching. When so fortunate as to have a new
listener, he began by telling him or her that
he was his father's fourth son, and conse-
quently third brother to Sir Grant Musselwhite—"who goes in so much for model-
farming, you know." At the hereditary
"place in Lincolnshire" he had spent the
bloom of his life, which he now looked back
upon with tender regrets. He did not
mention the fact that, at the age of five
and twenty, he had been beguiled from that
Arcadia by wily persons who took advantage
of his innocent youth, who initiated him
into the metropolitan mysteries which sadden the soul and deplete the pocket, who
finally abandoned him upon the shoal of a
youngest brother's allowance when his father
passed away from the place in Lincolnshire,

and young Sir Grant, reigning in the old
baronet's stead, deemed himself generous
in making the family scrapegrace any pro-
vision at all. Yet such were the outlines
of Mr. Musselwhite's history. Had he been
the commonplace spendthrift, one knows
pretty well on what lines his subsequent
life would have run; but poor Mr. Musselwhite was at heart a domestic creature.
Exiled from his home, he wandered in melancholy, year after year, round a circle of
continental resorts, never seeking relief in
dissipation, never discovering a rational
pursuit, imagining to himself that he atoned
for the disreputable past in keeping far from
the track of his distinguished relatives.

Ah, that place in Lincolnshire! To the
listener's mind it became one of the most
imposing of English ancestral abodes. The
house was of indescribable magnitude and
splendour. It had a remarkable "turret,"
whence, across I know not how many miles
of plain, Lincoln Cathedral could be discovered by the naked eye; it had an inter-

minable drive from the lodge to the stately
portico; it had gardens of fabulous fertility;
it had stables which would have served a
cavalry regiment. In what region were the
kine of Sir Grant Musselwhite unknown to
fame? Who had not heard of his dairy-
produce? Three stories was Mr. Musselwhite in the habit of telling, scintillating
fragments of his blissful youth; one was of
a fox-cub and a terrier; another of a heifer
that went mad; the third, and the most
thrilling, of a dismissed coachman who
turned burglar, and in the dead of night
fired shots at old Sir Grant and his sons.
In relating these anecdotes, his eye grew
moist and his throat swelled.

Mr. Musselwhite's place at table was next
to Barbara Denyer. So long as Miss Denyer
was new, or comparatively new, to her
neighbour's reminiscences, all went well
between them. Barbara condescended to
show interest in the place in Lincolnshire;
she put pertinent questions; she smiled or
looked appropriately serious in listening to

the three stories. But this could not go on
indefinitely, and for more than a week now
conversation between the two had been a
trying matter. For Mr. Musselwhite to
sustain a dialogue on such topics as Barbara
had made her own was impossible, and he
had no faculty even for the commonest kind
of impersonal talk. He devoted himself to
his dinner in amiable silence, enjoying the
consciousness that nearly an hour of occupation was before him, and that bed-time
lay at no hopeless distance.

A boy there was—yet I know not whether
I should so describe him; for, though he
numbered rather less than sixteen years,
experience had already made him *blasé*. He
sat beside his mother, a Mrs. Strangwich.
For Master Strangwich the ordinary sources
of youthful satisfaction did not exist; he
talked with the mature on terms of something more than equality, and always gave
them the impression that they had still
much to learn. This objectionable youth
had long since been everywhere and seen

everything. The *naïveté* of finding pleasure
in novel circumstances moved him to a pity-
ing surprise. Speak of the glories of the
Bay of Naples, and he would remark, with
hands in pockets and head thrown back,
that he thought a good deal more of the
Golden Horn. If climate came up for discussion, he gave an impartial vote, based
on much personal observation, in favour of
Southern California. His parents belonged
to the race of modern nomads, those curious
beings who are reviving an early stage of
civilization as an ingenious expedient for
employing money and time which they have
not intelligence enough to spend in a settled
habitat. It was already noticed in the
pension that Master Strangwich paid somewhat marked attentions to Madeline Denyer;
there was no knowing what might come
about if their acquaintance should be prolonged for a few weeks.

But Madeline had at present something
else to think about than the condescending
favour of Master Strangwich. As the guests

entered the dining-room, Madame Glück informed Mrs. Denyer that the English artist who was looked for had just arrived, and would in a few minutes join the company. " Mr. Marsh is here," said Mrs. Denyer aloud to her daughters, in a tone of no particular satisfaction. Madeline glanced at Miss Doran, who, however, did not seem to have heard the remark.

And, whilst the guests were still busy with their soup, Mr. Clifford Marsh presented himself. Within the doorway he stood for a moment surveying the room ; with placid eye he selected Mrs. Denyer, and approached her just to shake hands; her three daughters received from him the same attention. Words Mr. Marsh had none, but he smiled as smiles the man conscious of attracting merited observation. Indeed, it was impossible not to regard Mr. Marsh with curiosity. His attire was very conventional in itself, but somehow did not look like the evening uniform of common men : it sat upon him with an artistic freedom, and seemed the

garb of a man superior to his surroundings.
The artist was slight, pale, rather feminine
of feature; he had delicate hands, which he
managed to display to advantage; his auburn
hair was not long behind, as might have
been expected, but rolled in a magnificent
mass upon his brows, ambrosial, soul-shadow-
ing. Many were the affectations whereby
his countenance rendered itself unceasingly
interesting. At times he wrinkled his forehead down the middle, and then smiled at
vacancy—a humorous sadness; or his eyes
became very wide as he regarded, yet appeared not to see, some particular person;
or his lips drew themselves in, a symbol of
meaning reticence. All this, moreover, not
in such degrees as to make him patently
ridiculous; by no means. Mr. and Mrs.
Bradshaw might exchange frequent glances,
and have a difficulty in preserving decorum;
but then these were children of nature, and
would doubtless have indulged in profane
laughter at sight of an early portrait of
Alfred Tennyson. Mrs. Lessingham smiled,

indeed, when there came a reasonable pretext, but not contemptuously. Mr. Marsh's aspect, if anything, pleased her; she liked these avoidances of the commonplace. Cecily did not fail to inspect the new arrival. She too was well aware that hatred of vulgarity constrains many persons who are anything but fools to emphasize their being in odd ways, and it might still—in spite of the impressionist water-colours—be proved that Mr. Marsh had a right to vary from the kindly race of men. She hoped he was really a person of some account; it delighted her to be with such. And then she suspected that Madeline Denyer had something more than friendship for Mr. Marsh, and her sympathies were moved.

"What sort of weather did you leave in England?" Mrs. Denyer inquired, when the artist was seated next to her.

"I came away from London on the third day of absolute darkness," replied Mr. Marsh, genially.

"Oh dear!" exclaimed Madame Glück;

and at once translated this news for the benefit of Frau Wohlgemuth, who murmured, "Ach!" and shook her head.

"The fog is even yet in my throat," proceeded the artist, to whom most of the guests were listening. "I can still see nothing but lurid patches of gaslight on a background of solid, mephitic fume. There are fine effects to be caught, there's no denying it; but not every man has the requisite physique for such studies. As I came along here from the railway-station, it occurred to me that the Dante story might have been repeated in my case: the Neapolitans should have pointed at me and whispered, 'Behold the man who has been in hell!'"

Cecily was amused; she looked at Madeline and exchanged a friendly glance with her. At the same time she was becoming aware that Mr. Marsh, who sat opposite, vouchsafed her the homage of his gaze rather too frequently and persistently. It was soon manifest to her, moreover, that Madeline had noted the same thing, and not with entire equanimity. So Cecily began to converse with Mrs. Lessingham, and no longer gave heed to the artist's utterances.

She was going to spend an hour with Miriam this evening, without express invitation. Mr. Bradshaw would drive up the hill with her, and doubtless Mr. Spence would see her safely home. Thus she saw no more for the present of the Denyers' friend.

Those ladies had a private sitting-room, and thither, in the course of the evening, Clifford Marsh repaired. Barbara and Zillah, with their mother, remained in the drawing-room. On opening the door to which he had been directed, Marsh found Madeline bent over a book. She raised her eyes carelessly, and said :

" Oh, I hoped it was Barbara."

" I will tell her at once that you wish to speak to her."

" Don't trouble."

" No trouble at all."

He turned away, and at once Madeline

rose impatiently from her chair, speaking
with peremptory accent.

"Please do as I request you! Come and
sit down."

Marsh obeyed, and more than obeyed.
He kicked a stool close to her, dropped
upon it with one leg curled underneath him,
and leaned his head against her shoulder.
Madeline remained passive, her features still
showing the resentment his manner had
provoked.

"I've come all this way just to see you,
Mad, when I've no right to be here at
all."

"Why no right?"

"I told you to prepare yourself for bad
news."

"That's a very annoying habit of yours.
I hate to be kept in suspense in that way.
Why can't you always say at once what you
mean? Father does the same thing constantly in his letters. I'm sure we've quite
enough anxiety from him; I don't see why
you should increase it."

Without otherwise moving, he put his arm about her.

"What is it, Clifford? Tell me, and be quick."

"It's soon told, Mad. My step-father informs me that he will continue the usual allowance until my twenty-sixth birthday —eighteenth of February next, you know— and no longer than that. After then, I must look out for myself."

Madeline knit her brows.

"What's the reason?" she asked, after a pause.

"The old trouble. He says I've had quite long enough to make my way as an artist, if I'm going to make it at all. In his opinion, I am simply wasting my time and his money. No cash results; that is to say, no success. Of course, his view."

The girl kept silence. Marsh shifted his position slightly, so as to get a view of her face.

"Somebody else's too, I'm half afraid," he murmured dubiously.

Madeline was thinking of a look she had caught on Miss Doran's face when the portfolio disclosed its contents; of Miss Doran's silence; of certain other persons' looks and silence—or worse than silence. The knitting of her brows became deeper; Marsh felt an uneasy movement in her frame.

"Speak plainly," he said. "It's far better."

"It's very hot, Clifford. Sit on a chair; we can talk better."

"I understand."

He moved a little away from her, and looked round the room with a smile of disillusion.

"You needn't insult me," said Madeline, but not with the former petulance. "Often enough you have done that, and yet I don't think I have given you cause."

Still crouching upon the stool, he clasped his hands over his knee, jerked his head back—a frequent movement, to settle his hair—and smiled with increase of bitterness.

"I meant no insult," he said, "either now

or at other times, though you are always ready to interpret me in that way. I merely hint at the truth, which would sound disagreeable in plain terms."

"You mean, of course, that I think of nothing—have never thought of anything—but your material prospects?"

"Why didn't you marry me a year ago, Mad?"

"Because I should have been mad indeed to have done so. You admit it would have caused your step-father at once to stop his allowance. And pray what would have become of us?"

"Exactly. See your faith in me, brought to the touchstone!"

"I suppose the present day would have seen you as it now does?"

"Yes, if you had embarrassed me with lack of confidence. Decidedly not, if you had been to me the wife an artist needs. My future has lain in your power to make or mar. You have chosen to keep me in perpetual anxiety, and now you take a suit-

able opportunity to overthrow me altogether; or rather, you try to. We will
see how things go when I am free to pursue
my course untroubled."

"Do so, by all manner of means!" exclaimed Madeline, her voice trembling.
"Perhaps I shall prove to have been your
friend in this way, at all events. As your
wife in London lodgings on the third floor,
I confess it is very unlikely I should have
aided you. I haven't the least belief in projects of that kind. At best, you would have
been forced into some kind of paltry work
just to support me—and where would be the
good of our marriage? You know perfectly
well that lots of men have been degraded in
this way. They take a wife to be their
Muse, and she becomes the millstone about
their neck; then they hate her—and I don't
blame them. What's the good of saying
one moment that you know your work can
never appeal to the multitude, and the next,
affecting to believe that our marriage would
make you miraculously successful?"

"Then it would have been better to part before this."

"No doubt—as it turns out."

"Why do you speak bitterly? I am stating an obvious fact."

"If I remember rightly, you had some sort of idea that the fact of our engagement might help you. That didn't seem to me impossible. It is a very different thing from marriage on nothing a year."

"You have no faith in me; you never had. And how *could* you believe in what you don't understand? I see now what I have been forced to suspect—that your character is just as practical as that of other women. Your talk of art is nothing more than talk. You think, in truth, of pounds, shillings and pence."

"I think of them a good deal," said Madeline, "and I should be an idiot if I didn't. What is art if the artist has nothing to live on? Pray, what are *you* going to do henceforth? Shall you scorn the mention of pounds, shillings and pence? Come to see me when you have had no dinner to-day, and are feeling very uncertain about breakfast in the morning, and I will say, ' Pooh ! your talk about art was after all nothing but talk ; you are a sham !' "

Marsh's leg began to ache.   He rose and moved about the room.   Madeline at length turned her eyes to him ; he was brooding genuinely, and not for effect.   Her glance discerned this.

" Well, and what *are* you going to do, in fact ? " she asked.

" I'm hanged if I know, Mad ; and there's the truth."

He turned and regarded her with wide eyes, seriously perceptive of a blank horizon.

" I've asked him to let me have half the money, but he refuses even that.   His object is, of course, to compel me into the life of a Philistine.   I believe the fellow thinks it's kindness ; I know my mother does.   She, of course, has as little faith in me as you have."

Madeline did not resent this.   She regarded the floor for a minute, and, without raising her eyes, said :

"Come here, Clifford."

He approached. Still without raising her eyes, she again spoke.

"Do you believe in yourself?"

The words were impressive. Marsh gave a start, uttered an impatient sound, and half turned away.

"Do you believe in yourself, Clifford?"

"Of course I do!" came from him blusterously.

"Very well. In that case, struggle on. If you care for the kind of help you once said I could give you, I will try to give it still. Paint something that will sell, and go on with the other work at the same time."

"Something that will sell!" he exclaimed, with disgust. "I can't, so there's an end of it."

"And an end of your artist life, it seems to me. Unless you have any other plan?"

"I wondered whether you could suggest any."

Madeline shook her head slowly. They both brooded in a cheerless way. When the girl again spoke, it was in an undertone, as if not quite sure that she wished to be heard.

"I had rather you were an artist than anything else, Clifford."

Marsh decided not to hear. He thrust his hands deeper into his pockets, and trod about the floor heavily. Madeline made another remark.

"I suppose the kind of work that is proposed for you would leave you no time for art?"

"Pooh! of course not. Who was ever Philistine and artist at the same time?"

"Well, it's a bad job. I wish I could help you. I wish I had money."

"If you had, *I* shouldn't benefit by it," was the exasperated reply.

"Will you please to do what you were going to do at first, and tell Barbara I wish to speak to her?"

"Yes, I will."

His temper grew worse. In his weakness he really had thought it likely that Madeline would suggest something hopeful. Men of his stamp constantly entertain unreasonable expectations, and are angry when the unreason is forced upon their consciousness.

" One word before you go, please," said Madeline, standing up and speaking with emphasis. " After what you said just now, this is, of course, our last interview of this kind. When we meet again—and I think it would be gentlemanly in you to go and live somewhere else—you are Mr. Marsh, and I, if you please, am Miss Denyer."

" I will bear it in mind."

" Thank you." He still lingered near the door. " Be good enough to leave me."

He made an effort and left the room. When the door had closed, Madeline heaved a deep sigh, and was for some minutes in a brown, if not a black, study. Then she shivered a little, sighed again, and again took up the volume she had been reading. It was Daudet's " Les Femmes d'Artistes."

Not long after, all the Denyers were re-united in their sitting-room. Mrs. Denyer had brought up an open letter.

"From your father again," she said, addressing the girls conjointly. "I am sure he wears me out. This is worse than the last. 'The fact of the matter is, I must warn you very seriously that I can't supply you with as much as I have been doing. I repeat that I am serious this time. It's a horrible bore, and a good deal worse than a bore. If I could keep your remittances the same by doing on less myself, I would, but there's no possibility of that. I shall be in Alexandria in ten days, and perhaps Colossi will have some money for me, but I can't count on it. Things have gone deuced badly, and are likely to go even worse, as far as I can see. Do think about getting less expensive quarters. I wish to heaven poor little Mad could get married! Hasn't Marsh any prospects yet?'"

"That's all at an end," remarked Made line, interrupting. "We've just come to an understanding."

Mrs. Denyer stared.

" You've broken off ? "

" Mr. Marsh's allowance is to be stopped. His prospects are worse than ever. What's the good of keeping up our engagement ?"

There was a confused colloquy between all four. Barbara shrugged her fair shoulders ; Zillah looked very gravely and pitifully at Madeline. Madeline herself seemed the least concerned.

" I won't have this !" cried Mrs. Denyer, finally. " His step-father is willing to give him a position in business, and he must accept it ; then the marriage can be soon."

" The marriage will decidedly *not* be soon, mother !" replied Madeline, haughtily. " I shall judge for myself in this, at all events."

" You are a silly, empty-headed girl !" retorted her mother, with swelling bosom and reddening face. " You have quarrelled on some simpleton's question, no doubt. He will accept his step-father's offer ; we know that well enough. He ought to have done so a year ago, and our difficulties would have been lightened. Your father means what he says."

"Wolf!" cried Barbara, petulantly.

"Well, I can see that the wolf has come at last, in good earnest. My girl, you'll have to become more serious. Barbara, *you* at all events, cannot afford to trifle."

"I am no trifler!" cried the enthusiast for Italian unity and regeneracy.

"Let us have proof of that, then." Mrs. Denyer looked at her meaningly.

"Mother," said Zillah, earnestly, "do let me write to Mrs. Stonehouse, and beg her to find me a place as nursery governess. I can manage that, I feel sure."

"I'll think about it, dear. But, Madeline, I insist on your putting an end to this ridiculous state of things. You will *order* him to take the position offered."

"Mother, I can do nothing of the kind. If necessary, I'll go for a governess as well."

Thereupon Zillah wept, protesting that

such desecration was impossible. The scene prolonged itself to midnight. On the morrow, with the exception of Mrs. Denyer's resolve to subdue Marsh, all was forgotten, and the Denyer family pursued their old course, putting off decided action until there should come another cry of " Wolf ! "

CHAPTER IV.

MIRIAM'S BROTHER.

BUT for the aid of his wife's more sympathetic insight, Edward Spence would have continued to interpret Miriam's cheerless frame of mind as a mere result of impatience at being removed from the familiar scenes of her religious activity, and of disquietude amid uncongenial surroundings. "A Puritan at Naples"—that was the phrase which represented her to his imagination; his liking for the picturesque and suggestive led him to regard her solely in that light. No strain of modern humanitarianism complicated Miriam's character. One had not to take into account a possible melancholy produced by the contrast between her life of ease in the South, and the squalor of

laborious multitudes under a sky of mill-
smoke and English fog. Of the new philan-
thropy, she spoke, if at all, with angry scorn,
holding it to be based on rationalism,
radicalism, positivism, or whatsoever name
embodied the conflict between the children
of this world and the children of light. Far
from Miriam any desire to abolish the misery
which was among the divinely appointed
conditions of this preliminary existence.
No; she was uncomfortable, and content
that others should be so, for discomfort's
sake. It fretted her that the Sunday in
Naples could not be as universally dolorous
as it was at Bartles. It revolted her to
hear happy voices in a country abandoned
to heathendom.

"Whenever I see her looking at old
Vesuvius," said Spence to Eleanor, his eye
twinkling, "I feel sure that she muses on
the possibility of another tremendous out-
break. She regards him in a friendly way;
he is the minister of vengeance."

Eleanor's discernment was not long in

bringing her to a modification of this estimate.

"I am convinced, Ned, that her thoughts are not so constantly at Bartles as we imagine. In any case, I begin to understand what she suffers from most. It is want of occupation for her mind. She is crushed with *ennui*."

"This is irreverence. As well attribute *ennui* to the Prophet Jeremiah meditating woes to come."

"I allow you your joke, but I am right for all that. She has nothing to think about that profoundly interests her; her books are all but as sapless to her as to you or me. She is sinking into melancholia."

"But, my dear girl, the chapel!"

"She only pretends to think of it. Miriam is becoming a hypocrite; I have noted several little signs of it since Cecily came. She poses—and in wretchedness. Please to recollect that her age is four and twenty."

" I do so frequently, and marvel at human nature."

" I do so, and without marvelling at all, for I see human nature justifying itself. I'll tell you what I am going to do. I shall propose to her to begin and read Dante."

" The ' Inferno.' Why, yes."

" And I shall craftily introduce to her attention one or two wicked and worldly little books, such as ' The Improvisatore,' and the ' Golden Treasury,' and so on. Any such attempts at first would have been premature ; but I think the time has come."

Miriam knew no language but her own, and Eleanor by no means purposed inviting her to a course of grammar and exercise. She herself, with her husband's assistance, had learned to read Italian in the only rational way for mature-minded persons— simply taking the text and a close translation, and glancing from time to time at a skeleton accidence. This, of course, will not do in the case of fools, but Miriam Baske, all appearances notwithstanding, did not

belong to that category. On hearing her
cousin's proposition, she at first smiled
coldly; but she did not reject it, and in a
day or two they had made a fair beginning of the 'Inferno.' Such a beginning,
indeed, as surprised Eleanor, who was not
yet made aware that Miriam worked at
the book in private with feverish energy—
drank at the fountain like one perishing of
thirst. Andersen's exquisite story was not
so readily accepted, yet this too before long
showed a book-marker. And Miriam's
countenance brightened; she could not
conceal this effect. Her step was a little
lighter, and her speech became more
natural.

A relapse was to be expected; it came at
the bidding of scirocco. One morning the
heavens lowered, grey, rolling; it might
have been England. Vesuvius, heavily
laden at first with a cloud like that on
Olympus when the gods are wrathful, by
degrees passed from vision, withdrew its
form into recesses of dun mists. The angry

blue of Capri faded upon a troubled blending of sea and sky; everywhere the horizon contracted and grew mournful; rain began to fall.

Miriam sank as the heavens darkened. The strength of which she had lately been conscious forsook her; all her body was oppressed with languor, her mind miserably void. No book made appeal to her, and the sight of those which she had brought from home was intolerable. She lay upon a couch, her limbs torpid, burdensome. Eleanor's company was worse than useless.

"Please leave me alone," she said at length. "The sound of your voice irritates me."

An hour went by, and no one disturbed her mood. Her languor was on the confines of sleep, when a knock at the door caused her to stir impatiently and half raise herself. It was her maid, who entered, holding a note.

"A gentleman has called, ma'am. He wished me to give you this."

Miriam glanced at the address, and at once stood up, only her pale face witnessing to the lack of energy of a moment ago.

" Is he waiting ? "

" Yes, ma'am."

The note was of two or three lines: " Will you let me see you ? Of course I mean alone. It's a long time since we saw each other.—R. E."

" I will see him in this room."

The footstep of the maid as she came back along the tiled corridor was accompanied by one much heavier. Miriam kept her eyes turned to the door; her look was of pained expectancy and of sternness. She stood close by the window, as if purposely drawing as far away as possible. The visitor was introduced, and the door closed behind him.

He too stood still, as far from Miriam as might be. His age seemed to be seven or eight and twenty, and the cast of his features so strongly resembled Miriam's that there was no doubt of his being her

brother. Yet he had more beauty as a man
than she as a woman. Her traits were in
him developed so as to lose severity and
attain a kind of vigour, which at first sight
promised a rich and generous nature; his
excellent forehead and dark imaginative
eyes indicated a mind anything but likely
to bear the trammels in which Miriam had
grown up. In the attitude with which he
waited for his sister to speak there was
both pride and shame; his look fell before
hers, but the constrained smile on his lips
was one of self-esteem at issue with adversity. He wore the dress of a gentleman,
but it was disorderly. His light overcoat
hung unbuttoned, and in his hand he
crushed together a hat of soft felt.

"Why have you come to see me,
Reuben?" Miriam asked at length, speaking
with difficulty and in an offended tone.

"Why shouldn't I, Miriam?" he returned
quietly, stepping nearer to her. "Till a
few days ago I knew nothing of the illness
you have had, or I should, at all events,

have written. When I heard you had come to Naples, I—well, I followed. I might as well be here as anywhere else, and I felt a wish to see you."

"Why should you wish to see me? What does it matter to you whether I am well or ill?"

"Yes, it matters, though of course you find it hard to believe."

"Very, when I remember the words with which you last parted from me. If I was hateful to you then, how am I less so now?"

"A man in anger, and especially one of my nature, often says more than he means. It was never *you* that were hateful to me, though your beliefs and your circumstances might madden me into saying such a thing."

"My beliefs, as I told you then, are a part of myself—*are* myself."

She said it with irritable insistence—an accent which would doubtless have been significant in the ears of Eleanor Spence.

"I don't wish to speak of that. Have you recovered your health, Miriam?"

"I am better."

He came nearer again, throwing his hat aside.

"Will you let me sit down? I've had a long journey in third-class, and I feel tired. Such weather as this doesn't help to make me cheerful. I imagined Naples with a rather different sky."

Miriam motioned towards a chair, and looked drearily from the window at the dreary sea. Neither spoke again for two or three minutes. Reuben Elgar surveyed the room, but inattentively.

"What is it you want of me?" Miriam asked, facing him abruptly.

"Want? You hint that I have come to ask you for money?"

"I shouldn't have thought it impossible. If you were in need—you spoke of a third-class journey—I am, at all events, the natural person for your thoughts to turn to."

Reuben laughed dispiritedly.

"No, no, Miriam; I haven't quite got to that. You are the very last person I should think of in such a case."

"Why?"

"Simply because I am not quite so contemptible as you think me. I don't quarrel with my sister, and come back after some years to make it up just because I want to make a demand on her purse."

"You haven't accustomed me to credit you with high motives, Reuben."

"No. And I have never succeeded in making you understand me. I suppose it's hopeless that you ever will. We are too different. You regard me as a vulgar reprobate, who by some odd freak of nature happens to be akin to you. I can picture so well what your imagination makes of me. All the instances of debauchery and general blackguardism that the commerce of life has forced upon your knowledge go towards completing the ideal. It's a pity. I have always felt that you and I might have been a great deal to each other if you had had a reasonable education. I remember you as a child rebelling against the idiocies of your training, before your brain and soul had utterly yielded; then you were my sister, and even then, if it had been possible, I would have dragged you away and saved you."

"I thank Heaven," said Miriam, "that my childhood was in other hands than yours!"

"Yes; and it is very bitter to me to hear you say so."

Miriam kept silence, but looked at him less disdainfully.

"I suppose," he said, "the people you are staying with have much the same horror of my name as you have."

"You speak as loosely as you think. The Spences can scarcely respect you."

"You purpose remaining with them all the winter?"

"It is quite uncertain. With what intentions have you come here? Do you wish me to speak of you to the Spences or not?"

He still kept looking about the room. Perhaps upon him too the baleful southern wind was exercising its influence, for he sat listlessly when he was not speaking, and had a weary look.

"You may speak of me or not, as you like. I don't see that anything's to be gained by my meeting them; but I'll do just as you please."

"You mean to stay in Naples?"

"A short time. I've never been here before, and, as I said, I may as well be here as anywhere else."

"When did you last see Mr. Mallard?"

"Mallard? Why, what makes you speak of him?"

"You made his acquaintance, I think, not long after you last saw me."

"Ha! I understand. That was why he sought me out. You and your friends sent him to me as a companion likely to 'do me good.'"

"I knew nothing of Mr. Mallard then—nothing personally. But he doesn't seem to be the kind of man whose interest you would resent."

"Then you know him?" Reuben asked, in a tone of some pleasure.

"He is in Naples at present."

"I'm delighted to hear it. Mallard is an excellent fellow, in his own way. Somehow I've lost sight of him for a long time. He's painting here, I suppose? Where can I find him?"

"I don't know his address, but I can at once get it for you. You are sure that he will welcome you?"

"Why not? Have you spoken to him about me?"

"No," Miriam replied distantly.

"Why shouldn't he welcome me, then? We were very good friends. Do you attribute to him such judgments as your own?"

His way of speaking was subject to abrupt changes. When, as in this instance, he broke forth impulsively, there was a corresponding gleam in his fine eyes and a nervous tension in all his frame. His voice had an extraordinary power of conveying scornful passion ; at such moments he seemed to reveal a profound and strong nature.

"I am very slightly acquainted with Mr. Mallard," Miriam answered, with the cold austerity which was the counterpart in her of Reuben's fiery impulsiveness, "but I understand that he is considered trustworthy and honourable by people of like character."

Elgar rose from his chair, and in doing so all but flung it down.

"Trustworthy and honourable ! Why, so is many a greengrocer. How the artist would be flattered to hear this estimate of his personality ! The honourable Mallard ! I must tell him that."

"You will not dare to repeat words from my lips !" exclaimed Miriam, sternly. "You have sunk lower even than I thought."

"What limit, then, did you put to my debasement ? In what direction had I still a scrap of trustworthiness and honour left ? "

" Tell me that yourself, instead of talking to no purpose in this frenzied way. Why do you come here, if you only wish to renew our old differences ? "

" You were the first to do so."

" Can I pretend to be friendly with you, Reuben ? What word of penitence have you spoken ? In what have you amended yourself ? Is not every other sentence you speak a defence of yourself and scorn upon me ? "

" And what right have you to judge me ? Of course I defend myself, and as scornfully as you like, when I am despised and condemned by one who knows as little of me as the first stranger I pass on the road. Cannot you come forward with a face like a sister's, and leave my faults for my own conscience ? *You* judge me ! What do you, with your nun's experiences, your heart chilled, your paltry view of the world through a chapel window, know of a man whose passions boil in him like the fire in yonder mountain ? I should subdue my

passions. Excellent text for a copy-book
in a girls' school! I should be another man
than I am; I should remould myself; I
should cool my brain with doctrine. With
a bullet, if you like; say that, and you will
tell the truth. But with the truth you have
nothing to do; too long ago you were
taught that you must never face that. Do
you deal as truthfully with yourself as I
with my own heart? I wonder, I wonder."

Miriam's eyes had fallen. She stood
quite motionless, with a face of suffering.

"You want me to confess my sins?"
Reuben continued, walking about in uncon-
trollable excitement. "What is your chapel
formula? Find one comprehensive enough,
and let me repeat it after you; only mind
that it includes hypocrisy, for the sake of
the confession. I tell you I am conscious
of no sins. Of follies, of ignorances, of
miseries—as many as you please. And to
what account should they all go? Was I
so admirably guided in childhood and boyhood that my subsequent life is not to be

explained? It succeeded in your case, my
poor sister. Oh, nobly! Don't be afraid
that I shall outrage you by saying all I
think. But just think of *me* as a result of
Jewish education applied to an English lad,
and one whose temperament was plain
enough to eyes of ordinary penetration.
My very name! Your name, too! You it
has made a Jew in soul; upon me it weighs
like a curse as often as I think of it. It
symbolizes all that is making my life a
brutal failure—a failure—a failure!"

He threw himself upon the couch and
became silent, his strength at an end, even
his countenance exhausted of vitality, looking haggard and almost ignoble. Miriam
stirred at length, for the first time, and
gazed steadily at him.

"Reuben, let us have an end of this," she
said, in a voice half choked. "Stay or go
as you will; but I shall utter no more
reproaches. You must make of your life
what you can. As you say, I don't understand you. Perhaps the mere fact of my

being a woman is enough to make that impossible. Only don't throw your scorn at me for believing what you can't believe. Talk quietly; avoid those subjects; tell me, if you wish to, what you are doing or think of doing."

"You should have spoken like this earlier, Miriam. It would have spared my memory its most wretched burden."

"How?"

"You know quite well that I valued your affection, and that it had no little importance in my life. Instead of still having my sister, I had only the memory of her anger and injustice, and of my own cursed temper."

"I had no influence for good."

"Perhaps not in the common sense of the words. I am not going to talk humbug about a woman's power to make a man angelic; that will do for third-rate novels and plays. But I shouldn't have thrown myself away as I have done if you had cared to know what I was doing."

"Did I not care, Reuben?"

" If so, you thought it was your duty not to show it. You thought harshness was the only proper treatment for a case such as mine. I had had too much of that."

" What did you mean just now by speaking as though you were poor ? "

" I have been poor for a long time—poor compared with what I was. Most of my money has gone—on the fool's way. I haven't come here to lament over it. It's one of my rules never, if I can help it, to think of the past. What has been, has been ; and what will be, will be. When I fume and rage like an idiot, that's only the blood in me getting the better of the brain ; an example of the fault that always wrecks me. Do you think I cannot see myself ? Just now, I couldn't keep back the insensate words—insensate because useless—but I judged myself all the time as distinctly as I do now it's over."

" Your money gone, Reuben ? " murmured his sister, in consternation.

" You might have foreseen that. Come

and sit down by me, Miriam. I am tired
and wretched. Where is the sun? Surely
one may have sunshine at Naples!"

He was now idly fretful. Miriam seated
herself at his side, and he took her hand.

"I thought you might perhaps receive
me like this at first. I came only with that
hope. I wish you looked better, Miriam.
How do you employ yourself here?"

"I am much out of doors. I get stronger."

"You spoke of old Mallard. I'm glad he
is here, really glad. You know, Mallard's
a fellow of no slight account; I should
think you might even like him."

"But yourself, Reuben?"

"No, no; let me rest a little. I'm sick
and tired of myself. Let's talk of old
Mallard. And what's become of little
Cecily Doran?"

"She is here—with her aunt."

"She here too! By Jove! Well, of
course I shall have nothing to do with them.
Mallard still acting as her guardian, I
suppose. Rather a joke, that. I never

could get him to speak on the subject. But I feel glad you know him. He's a solid fellow, tremendously conscientious; just the things you would like in a man, no doubt. Have you seen any of his painting?"

Miriam shook her head absently, unable to find voice for the topic, which was remote from her thoughts.

"He's done fine things, great things. I shall look him up, and we'll drink a bottle of wine together."

He kept stroking Miriam's hand, a white hand with blue veins—a strong hand, though so delicately fashioned. The touch of the wedding-ring again gave a new direction to his discursive thoughts.

"After this, shall you go back to that horrible hole in Lancashire?"

"I hope to go back home, certainly."

"Home, home!" he muttered impatiently. "It has made you ill, poor girl. Stay in Italy a long time, now you are once here. For you to be here at all seems a miracle; it gives me hopes."

Miriam did not resent this, in word at all events. She was submitting again to physical oppression; her head drooped, and her abstracted gaze was veiled with despondent lassitude. Reuben talked idly, in loose sentences.

"Do you think of me as old or young, Miriam?" he asked, when both had kept silence for a while.

"I no longer think of you as older than myself."

"That is natural. I imagined that. In one way I am old enough, but in another I am only just beginning my life, and have all my energies fresh. I shall do something yet; can you believe it?"

"Do what?" she asked wearily.

"Oh, I have plans; all sorts of plans."

He joined his hands together behind his head, and began to stir with a revival of mental energy.

"But plans of what sort?"

"There is only one direction open to me. My law has of course gone to—to limbo; it

was always an absurdity. Most of my
money has gone the same way, and I'm not
sorry for it. If I had never had anything,
I should have set desperately to work long
ago. Now I am bound to work, and you
will see the results. Of course, in our days,
there's only one road for a man like me. I
shall go in for literature."

Miriam listened, but made no comment.

"My life hitherto has not been wasted,"
Elgar pursued, leaning forward with a new
light on his countenance. "I have been
gaining experience. Do you understand?
Few men at my age have seen more of life
—the kind of life that is useful as literary
material. It's only quite of late that I have
begun to appreciate this, to see all the possibilities that are in myself. It has taken
all this time to outgrow the miserable mis-
direction of my boyhood, and to become a
man of my time. Thank the fates, I no longer
live in the Pentateuch, but at the latter end
of the nineteenth century. Many a lad has
to work this deliverance for himself nowa-

days. I don't wish to speak unkindly any more, Miriam, but I must tell you plain facts. Some fellows free themselves by dint of hard study. In my case that was made impossible by all sorts of reasons—temperament mainly, as you know. I was always a rebel against my fetters; I had not to learn that liberty was desirable, but how to obtain it, and what use to make of it. All the disorder through which I have gone was a struggle towards self-knowledge and understanding of my time. You and others are wildly in error in calling it dissipation, profligacy, recklessness, and so on. You at least, Miriam, ought to have judged me more truly; you, at all events, should not have classed me with common men."

His eyes were now agleam, and the beauty of his countenance fully manifest. He held his head in a pose of superb confidence. There was too much real force in his features to make this seem a demonstration of idle vanity. Miriam regarded him, and continued to do so.

" To be sure, my powers are in your eyes valueless," he pursued ; " or rather, your eyes have never been opened to anything of the kind. The nineteenth century is nothing to you ; its special opportunities and demands and characteristics would revolt you if they were made clear to your intelligence. If I tell you I am before everything a man of my time, I suppose this seems only a cynical confession of all the weaknesses and crimes you have already attributed to me ? It shall not always be so ! Why, what are you, after all, Miriam ? Twenty-three, twenty-four—which is it ? Why, you are a child still; your time of education is before you. You are a child come to Italy to learn what can be made of life ! "

She averted her face, but smiled, and not quite so coldly as of wont. She could not but think of Cecily, whose words a few days ago had been in spirit so like these, so like them in the ring of enthusiasm.

" Some day," Elgar went on, exalting

himself more and more, "you shall wonder in looking back on this scene between us— wonder how you could have been so harsh to me. It is impossible that you and I, sole brother and sister, should move on constantly diverging paths. Tell me—you are not really without some kind of faith in my abilities?"

"You know it has always been my grief that you put them to no use."

"Very well. But it remains for you to learn what my powers really are, and to bring yourself to sympathize with my direction. You are a child—there is my hope. You shall be taught—yes, yes! Your obstinacy shall be overcome; you shall be made to see your own good!"

"And who is to be so kind as to take charge of my education?" Miriam asked, without looking at him, in an idly contemptuous tone.

"Why not old Mallard?" cried Reuben, breaking suddenly into jest. "The tutorship of children is in his line."

Miriam showed herself offended.

" Please don't speak of me. I am willing to hear what you purpose for yourself, but don't mix my name with it."

Elgar resumed the tone of ambition. Whether he had in truth definite literary schemes could not be gathered from the rhetoric on which he was borne. His main conviction seemed to be that he embodied the spirit of his time, and would ere long achieve a work of notable significance, the fruit of all his experiences. Miriam, though with no sign of strong interest, gave him her full attention.

" Do you intend to work here ? " she asked at length.

" I can't say. At present I am anything but well, and I shall get what benefit I can from Naples first of all. I suppose the sun will shine again before long ? This sky is depressing."

He stood up, and went to the windows; then came back with uncertain step.

" You'll tell the Spences I've been ? "

"I think I had better. They will know, of course, that I have had a visitor."

"Should I see them?" he asked, with hesitation.

"Just as you please."

"I shall have to, sooner or later. Why not now?"

Miriam pondered.

"I'll go and see if they are at leisure."

During her absence, Elgar examined the books on the table. He turned over each one with angry mutterings. The chapel plans were no longer lying about; only yesterday Miriam had rolled them up and put them away—temporarily. Before the "St. Cecilia" he stood in thoughtful observation, and was still there when Miriam returned. She had a look of uneasiness.

"Miss Doran and her aunt are with Mrs. Spence, Reuben."

"Oh, in that case——" he began carelessly, with a wave of the arm.

"But they will be glad to see you."

"Indeed? I look rather seedy, I'm afraid."

"Take off your overcoat."

"I'm all grimy. I came here straight from the railway."

"Then go into my bedroom and make yourself presentable."

A few moments sufficed for this. As she waited for his return, Miriam stood with knitted brows, her eyes fixed on the floor. Reuben reappeared, and she examined him.

"You're bitterly ashamed of me, Miriam."

She made no reply, and at once led the way along the corridor.

Mrs. Spence had met Reuben in London, since her marriage; by invitation he came to her house, but neglected to repeat the visit. To Mrs. Lessingham he was personally a stranger. But neither of these ladies received the honour of much attention from him for the first few moments after he had entered the room; his eyes and thoughts were occupied with the wholly unexpected figure of Cecily Doran. In his recollection, she was a slight, pale, shy little girl, fond of keeping in corners with a book, and seem-

ingly marked out for a life of dissenting
piety and provincial surroundings. She had
interested him little in those days, and
seldom did anything to bring herself under
his notice. He last saw her when she was
about twelve. Now he found himself in
the presence of a beautiful woman, every
line of whose countenance told of instruction, thought, spirit; whose bearing was
refined beyond anything he had yet understood by that word; whose modest revival
of old acquaintance made his hand thrill at
her touch, and his heart beat confusedly as
he looked into her eyes. With difficulty
he constrained himself to common social
necessities, and made show of conversing
with the elder ladies. He wished to gaze
steadily at the girl's face, and connect past
with present; to revive his memory of six
years ago, and convince himself that such
development was possible. At the same
time he became aware of a reciprocal curiosity in Cecily. When he turned towards
her she met his glance, and when he spoke

she gave him a smile of pleased attentiveness. The consequence was that he soon began to speak freely, to pick his words, to balance his sentences and shun the commonplace.

"I saw Florence and Rome in '76," he replied to a question from Mrs. Lessingham. "In Rome my travelling companion fell ill, and we returned without coming further south. It is wrong, however, to say that I *saw* anything; my mind was in far too crude a state to direct my eyes to any purpose. I stared about me a good deal, and got some notions of topography, and there the matter ended for the time."

"The benefit came with subsequent reflection, no doubt," said Mrs. Lessingham, who found one of her greatest pleasures in listening to the talk of young men with brains. Whenever it was possible, she gathered such individuals about her and encouraged them to discourse of themselves, generally quite as much to their satisfaction as to her own. Already she had invited with some success the confidence of Mr. Clifford Marsh, who proved interesting, but not unfathomable ; he belonged to a class with which she was tolerably familiar. Reuben Elgar, she perceived at once, was not without characteristics linking him to that same group of the new generation, but it seemed probable that its confines were too narrow for him. There was comparatively little affectation in his manner, and none in his aspect; his voice rang with a sincerity which claimed serious audience, and his eyes had something more than surface gleamings. Possibly he belonged to the unclassed and the unclassable, in which case the interest attaching to him was of the highest kind.

"Subsequent reflection," returned Elgar, "has, at all events, enabled me to see myself as I then was; and I suppose self-knowledge is the best result of travel."

"If one agrees that self-knowledge is ever a good at all," said the speculative lady, with her impartial smile.

"To be sure." Elgar looked keenly at her, probing the significance of the remark. "The happy human being will make each stage of his journey a phase of more or less sensual enjoyment, delightful at the time and valuable in memory. The excursion will be his life in little. I envy him, but I can't imitate him."

"Why envy him?" asked Eleanor.

"Because he is happy; surely a sufficient ground."

"Yet you give the preference to self-knowledge."

"Yes, I do. Because in that direction my own nature tends to develop itself. But I envy every lower thing in creation. I won't pretend to say how it is with other people who are forced along an upward path; in my own case every step is made with a groan, and why shouldn't I confess it?"

"To do so enhances the merit of progress," observed Mrs. Lessingham, mischievously.

"Merit? I know nothing of merit. I spoke of myself being *forced* upwards. If ever I feel that I am slipping back, I shall state it with just as little admission of shame."

Miriam heard this modern dialogue with grave features. At Bartles, such talk would have qualified the talker for social excommunication, and every other pain and penalty Bartles had in its power to inflict. She observed that Cecily's interest increased. The girl listened frankly; no sense of anything improper appeared in her visage. Nay, she was about to interpose a remark.

"Isn't there a hope, Mr. Elgar, that this envy of which you speak will be one of the things that the upward path leaves behind?"

"I should like to believe it, Miss Doran," he answered, his eyes kindling at hers. "It's true that I haven't yet gone very far."

"I like so much to believe it that I *do* believe it," the girl continued impulsively.

" Your progress in that direction exceeds mine."

" Don't be troubled by the compliment," interjected Eleanor, before Cecily could speak. " There is no question of merit."

Mrs. Lessingham laughed.

The rain still fell, and the grey heavens showed no breaking. Shortly after this, Elgar would have risen to take his leave, but Mrs. Spence begged him to remain and lunch with them. The visitors from the Mergellina declined a similar invitation.

Edward Spence was passing his morning at the Museum. On his return at luncheon-time, Eleanor met him with the intelligence that Reuben Elgar had presented himself, and was now in his sister's room.

" *In forma pauperis*, presumably," said Spence, raising his eyebrows.

" I can't say, but I fear it isn't impossible. Cecily and her aunt happened to call this morning, and he had some talk with them."

"Is he very much of a blackguard?" inquired her husband, disinterestedly.

"Indeed, no. That is to say, externally and in his conversation. It's a decided improvement on our old impressions of him."

"I'm glad to hear it," was the dry response.

"He has formed himself in some degree. Hints that he is going to produce literature."

"Of course." Spence laughed merrily. "The last refuge of a scoundrel."

"I don't like to judge him so harshly, Ned. He has a fine face."

"And is Miriam killing the fatted calf?"

"His arrival seems to embarrass rather than delight her."

"Depend upon it, the fellow has come to propose a convenient division of her personal property."

When he again appeared, Elgar was in excellent spirits. He met Spence with irresistible frankness and courtesy; his talk made the luncheon cheery, and dismissed thought of scirocco. It appeared that he had as yet no abode; his luggage was at the station. A suggestion that he should seek quarters under the same roof with Mallard recommended itself to him.

"I feel like a giant refreshed," he declared, in privately taking leave of Miriam. "Coming to Naples was an inspiration."

She raised her lips to his for the first time, but said nothing.

CHAPTER V.

THE ARTIST ASTRAY.

FROM the Strada di Chiaia, the narrow street winding between immense houses, all day long congested with the merry tumult of Neapolitan traffic, where herds of goats and milch cows placidly make their way among vehicles of every possible and impossible description; where *cocchieri* crack their whips and belabour their hapless cattle, and yell their "Ah—h—h! Ah h—h!"—where teams of horse, ox, and ass, the three abreast, drag piles of country produce, jingling their fantastic harness, and primitive carts laden with red-soaked wine-casks rattle recklessly along; where bare-footed, girdled, and tonsured monks plod on their no-business, and every third man you pass

is a rotund ecclesiastic, who never in his
life walked at more than a mile an hour;
where, at evening, carriages returning from
the Villa Nazionale cram the thoroughfare
from side to side, and make you aware, if
you did not previously know it, that parts
of the street have no pedestrians' pave-
ment;—from the Strada di Chiaia (now
doomed, alas ! by the exigencies of *lo sven-
tramento* and *il risanamento*) turn into the
public staircase and climb through the
dusk, with all possible attention to where
you set your foot, past the unmelodious
beggars, to the Ponte di Chiaia, bridge
which spans the roadway and looks down
upon its crowd and clamour as into a profound valley ; thence proceed uphill on the
lava paving, between fruit-shops and
sausage-shops and wine-shops, always in
an atmosphere of fried oil and roasted
chestnuts and baked pine-cones ; and presently turn left into a still narrower street,
with tailors and boot-makers and smiths
all at work in the open air ; and pass

through the Piazzetta Mondragone, and turn again to the left, but this time downhill; then lose yourself amid filthy little alleys, where the scent of oil and chestnuts and pine-cones is stronger than ever; then emerge on a little terrace where there is a noble view of the bay and of Capri; then turn abruptly between walls overhung with fig-trees and orange-trees and lemon-trees, —and you will reach Casa Rolandi.

It is an enormous house, with a great arched entrance admitting you to the inner court, where on the wall is a Madonna's shrine, lamp-illumined of evenings. A great staircase leads up from floor to floor. On each storey are two tenements, the doors facing each other. At the time of which I write, one of the apartments at the very top—an ascent equal to that of a moderate mountain—was in the possession of a certain Signora Bassano, whose name you might read engraven on a brass plate. This lady had furnished rooms to let, and here it was that our friend Ross Mallard had established himself for the few days that he proposed to spend in Naples.

Already he had lingered till the few days were become more than a fortnight, and still the day of his departure was undetermined. This was most unwonted waste of time, not easily accounted for by Mallard himself. A morning of sunny splendour, coming after much cloudiness and a good deal of rain, plucked him early out of bed, strong in the resolve that to-morrow should see him on the road to Amalfi. He had slept well—an exception in the past week—and his mind was open to the influences of sunlight and reason. Before going forth for breakfast he had a letter to write, a brief account of himself addressed to the vile little town of Sowerby Bridge, in Yorkshire. This finished, he threw open the big windows, stepped out on to the balcony, and drank deep draughts of air from the sea. In the street below was passing a flock of she-goats, all ready to be milked, each with a bell tinkling about her neck.

The goatherd kept summoning his customers with a long musical whistle. Mallard leaned over and watched the clean-fleeced, slender, graceful animals with a smile of pleasure. Then he amused himself with something that was going on in the house opposite. A woman came out on to a balcony high up, bent over it, and called "Annina! Annina!" until the call brought another woman on to the balcony immediately below; whereupon the former let down a cord, and her friend, catching the end of it, made it fast to a basket which contained food covered with a cloth. The basket was drawn up, the women gossipped and laughed for a while in pleasant voices, then they disappeared. All around, the familiar Neapolitan clamour was beginning. Church bells were ringing as they ring at Naples—a great crash, followed by a rapid succession of quivering little shakes, then the crash again. Hawkers were crying fruit and vegetables and fish in rhythmic cadence; a donkey was braying obstreperously.

Mallard had just taken a light overcoat on his arm, and was ready to set out, when some one knocked. He turned the key in the door, and admitted Reuben Elgar.

"I'm off to Pompeii," said Elgar, vivaciously.

"All right. You'll go to the 'Sole'? I shall be there myself to-morrow evening."

"I'm likely to stay several days, so we shall have more talk."

They left the house together, and presently parted with renewed assurance of meeting again on the morrow.

Mallard went his way thoughtfully, the smile quickly passing from his face. At a little *caffè*, known to him of old, he made a simple breakfast, glancing the while over a morning newspaper, and watching the children who came to fetch their *due soldi* of coffee in tiny cans. Then he strolled away and supplemented his meal with a fine bunch of grapes, bought for a penny at a stall that glowed and was fragrant with piles of fruit. Heedless of the carriage-drivers who shouted at him and even dogged him along street after street, he sauntered in the broad sunshine, plucking off his grapes and relishing them. Coming out by the sea-shore, he stood for a while to watch the fishermen dragging in their nets —picturesque fellows with swarthy faces and sun-tanned legs of admirable outline, hauling slowly in files at interminable rope, which boys coiled lazily as it came in ; or the oyster-dredgers, poised on the side of their boats over the blue water. At the foot of the sea-wall tumbled the tideless breakers ; their drowsy music counselled enjoyment of the hour and carelessness of what might come hereafter.

With no definite purpose, he walked on and on, for the most part absorbed in thought. He passed through the long *grotta* of Posilipo, gloomy, chilly, and dank ; then out again into the sunshine, and along the road to Bagnoli. On walls and stone-heaps the little lizards darted about, innumerable ; in vineyards men were at work dismantling the vine-props, often singing at their task. From Bagnoli, still walking merely that a movement of his limbs might accompany his busy thoughts, he went along by the sea-shore, and so at length, still long before midday, had come to Pozzuoli. A sharp conflict with the swarm of guides who beset the entrance to the town, and again he escaped into quietness, wandered among narrow streets, between blue, red, and yellow houses, stopping at times to look at some sunny upper window hung about with clusters of *sorbe* and *pomidori*. By this time he had won appetite for a more substantial meal. In the kind of eating-house that suited his mood, an obscure *bettola* probably never yet patronized by Englishman, he sat down to a dish of maccheroni and a bottle of red wine. At another table were some boatmen, who, after greeting him, went on with their lively talk in a dialect of which he could understand but few words.

Having eaten well and drunk still better, he lit a cigar and sauntered forth to find a place for dreaming. Chance led him to the patch of public garden, with its shrubs and young palm-trees, which looks over the little port. Here, when once he had made it clear to a succession of rhetorical boatmen that he was not to be tempted on to the sea, he could sit as idly and as long as he liked, looking across the sapphire bay and watching the bright sails glide hither and thither. With the help of sunlight and red wine, he could imagine (that time had gone back twenty centuries—that this was not Pozzuoli, but Puteoli; that over yonder was not Baia, but Baiæ; that the men among the shipping called to each other in Latin, and perchance had just heard some news of the perishing Republic.)

But Mallard's fancy would not dwell long in remote ages. As he watched the smoke curling up from his cigar, he slipped back into the world of his active being, and made no effort to obscure the faces that looked upon him. They were those of his mother and sisters, thought of whom carried him to

the northern island, now grim, cold, and
sunless beneath its lowering sky. These
relatives still lived where his boyhood had
been passed, a life strangely unlike his own,
and even alien to his sympathies, but their
house was still all that he could call home.
Was it to be always the same?

Fifteen years now, since, at the age of
twenty, he painted his first considerable
landscape, a tract of moorland on the borders
of Lancashire and Yorkshire. This was his
native ground. At Sowerby Bridge, a manu-
facturing town, which, like many others in
the same part of England, makes a blot
of hideousness on country in itself sternly
beautiful, his father had settled as the
manager of certain rope-works. Mr. Mallard's state was not unprosperous, for he had
invented a process put in use by his em-
ployers, and derived benefit from it. He
was a man of habitual gravity, occasionally
severe in the rule of his household, very
seldom unbending to mirthfulness. Though
not particularly robust, he employed his

leisure in long walks about the moors, walks sometimes prolonged till after midnight, sometimes begun long before dawn. His acquaintances called him unsociable, and doubtless he was so in the sense that he could not find at Sowerby Bridge any one for whose society he greatly cared. It was even a rare thing for him to sit down with his wife and children for more than a few minutes; if he remained in the house, he kept apart in a room of his own, musing over, rather than reading, a little collection of books—one of his favourites being Defoe's "History of the Devil." He often made ironical remarks, and seemed to have a grim satisfaction when his hearers missed the point. Then he would chuckle, and shake his head, and go away muttering.

Young Ross, who made no brilliant figure at school, and showed a turn for drawing, was sent at seventeen to the factory of Messrs. Gilstead, Miles and Doran, to become a designer of patterns. The result was something more than his father had

expected, for Mr. Doran, who had his abode
at Sowerby Bridge, almost at once discovered
that the lad was meant for far other things,
and, by dint of personal intervention, caused
Mr. Mallard to give his son a chance of
becoming an artist.

A remarkable man, this Mr. Doran. By
nature a Bohemian, somehow made into a
Yorkshire mill-owner; a strong, active, nobly
featured man, who dressed as no one in the
factory regions ever did before or probably
ever will again—his usual appearance suggesting the common notion of a bushranger;
an artist to the core ; a purchaser of pictures
by unknown men who had a future—at the
sale of his collection three Robert Cheeles
got into the hands of dealers, all of them
now the boasted possessions of great galleries;
a passionate lover of music—he had been
known to make the journey to Paris merely
to hear Diodati sing ; finally, in common
rumour a profligate whom no prudent house-
holder would admit to the society of his
wife and daughters. However, at the time

of young Mallard's coming under his notice
he had been married about a year. Mrs.
Doran came from Manchester; she was very
beautiful, but had slight education, and
before long Sowerby Bridge remarked that
the husband was too often away from home.

Doran and the elder Mallard, having
once met, were disposed to see more of each
other; in spite of the difference of social
standing, they became intimates, and Mr.
Mallard had at length some one with whom
he found pleasure in conversing. He did
not long enjoy the new experience. In the
winter that followed, he died of a cold contracted on one of his long walks when the
hills were deep in snow.

Doran remained the firm friend of the
family. Local talk had inspired Mrs. Mallard with a prejudice against him, but substantial services mitigated this, and the
widow was in course of time less uneasy
at her son's being in a manner under the
guardianship of this singular man of business. Mallard, after preliminary training,

was sent to the studio of a young artist
whom Doran greatly admired, Cullen Banks,
then struggling for the recognition he was
never to enjoy, death being beforehand with
him. Mrs. Mallard was given to understand
that no expenses were involved save those
of the lad's support in Manchester, where
Banks lived, and Mallard himself did not till
long after know that his friend had paid the
artist a fee out of his own pocket. Two
things did Mallard learn from Doran himself
which were to have a marked influence on
his life—a belief that only in landscape can
a painter of our time hope to do really great
work, and a limitless contempt of the Royal
Academy. In Manchester he made the
acquaintance of several people with whom
Doran was familiar, among them Edward
Spence, then in the shipping-office, and
Jacob Bush Bradshaw, well on his way to
making a fortune out of silk. On Banks's
death, Mallard, now nearly twenty-one, went
to London for a time. His patrimony was
modest, but happily, if the capital remained

intact, sufficient to save him from the cares
that degrade and waste a life. His mother
and sisters had also an income adequate to
their simple habits.

In the mean time, Mrs. Doran was dead.
After giving birth to a daughter, she fell
into miserable health; her husband took her
abroad, and she died in Germany. There-
after Sowerby Bridge saw no more of its
bugbear; Doran abandoned commerce and
became a Bohemian in earnest—save that
his dinner was always assured. He wandered all over Europe; he lived with Bohemian society in every capital; he kept
adding to his collection of pictures (stored in
a house at Woolwich, which he freely lent
as an abode to a succession of ill-to-do
artists); and finally he was struck with
paralysis whilst conducting to their home
the widow and child of a young painter who
had suddenly died in the Ardennes. The
poor woman under his protection had to
become his guardian. He was brought to the
house at Woolwich, and there for several

months lay between life and death. A partial recovery followed, and he was taken to the Isle of Wight, where, in a short time, a second attack killed him.

His child, Cecily, was twelve years old· For the last five years she had been living in the care of Mrs. Elgar at Manchester. This lady was an intimate friend of Mrs. Doran's family, and in entrusting his child to her, Doran had given a strong illustration of one of the singularities of his character. Though by no means the debauchee that Sowerby Bridge declared him, he was not a man of conventional morality; yet, in the case of people who were in any way intrusted to his care, he showed a curious severity of practice. Ross Mallard, for instance; no provincial Puritan could have instructed the lad more strenuously in the accepted moral code than did Mr. Doran on taking him from home to live in Manchester. In choosing a wife, he went to a family of conventional Dissenters; and he desired his daughter to pass the years of her childhood with people who he knew would guide her in the very straitest way of Puritan doctrine. What his theory was in this matter (if he had one) he told nobody. Dying, he made the dispositions of which you are already aware, leaving it to the discretion of the two trustees to appoint a residence for Cecily, if for any reason she could not remain with Mrs. Elgar. This occasion, as you know, soon presented itself, and Cecily passed into the care of Doran's sister, Mrs. Lessingham, who was just entered upon a happy widowhood. Mallard, most unexpectedly left sole trustee, had no choice but to assent to this arrangement ; the only other home possible for the girl was with Miriam at Redbeck House, but Mr. Baske did not look with favour on that proposal. Hitherto, Mr. Trench, the elder trustee, who lived in Manchester, had alone been in personal relations with Mrs. Elgar and little Cecily ; even now Mallard did not make the personal acquaintance of Mrs. Elgar (otherwise he would doubtless have met Miriam), but saw Mrs. Lessingham in London, and for the first time met Cecily when she came to the south in her aunt's care. He knew what an extreme change would be made in the manner of the girl's education, and it gave him some mental trouble; but it was clear that Cecily might benefit greatly in health by travel, and, as for the moral question, Mrs. Lessingham strongly stirred his sympathies by the dolorous account she gave of the child's surroundings in the north. Cecily was being intellectually starved; that seemed clear to Mallard himself after a little conversation with her. It was wonderful how much she had already learnt, impelled by sheer inner necessity, of things which in general she was discouraged from studying. So Cecily left England, to return only for short intervals, spent in London. Between that departure and this present meeting, Mallard saw her only twice; but Cecily had written to him with some regularity. These letters grew more and more delightful.

Cecily addressed herself with exquisite girlish frankness as to an old friend, old in both senses of the word ; collected, they made a history of her rapidly growing mind such as the shy artist might have gloried in possessing. In reality, he did nothing of the kind ; he wished the letters would not come and disturb him in his work. He sent gruff little answers, over which Cecily laughed, as so characteristic.

Yes, there was a distinct connection between those homely memories and picturings which took him in thought to Sowerby Bridge, and the image of Cecily Doran which had caused him to waste all this time in Naples. They represented two worlds, in both of which he had some part ; but it was only too certain with which of them he was the more closely linked. What but mere accident put him in contact with the world which was Cecily's ? Through her aunt she had aristocratic relatives ; her wealth made her a natural member of what is called society ; her beauty and her brilliancy marked her to be one of society's ornaments. What could she possibly be to him, Ross Mallard, landscape-painter of small if any note, as unaristocratic in mind and person as any one that breathed? To put the point with uncompromising plainness, and therefore in all its absurdity, how could he possibly imagine Cecily Doran called Mrs. Mallard?

The thing was flagrantly, grossly, palpably absurd. He tingled in the ears in trying to represent to himself how Cecily would think of it, if by any misfortune it were ever suggested to her.

Then why not, in the name of common sense, cease to ponder such follies, and get on with the work which waited for him? Why this fluttering about a flame which scorched him more and more dangerously? It was not the first time that he had experienced temptations of this kind; a story of five years ago, its scene in London, should have reminded him that he could stand a desperate wrench when convinced that his life's purpose depended upon it. Here were three years of trusteeship before him—he could not, or would not, count on her marrying before she came of age. Her letters would still come; from time to time doubtless he must meet her. It had all resulted from this confounded journey taken together! Why, knowing himself sufficiently, did he consent to meet the people at Genoa, loitering there for a couple of days in expectancy? Why had he come to Italy at all just now?

The answers to all such angry queries were plain enough, however he had hitherto tried to avoid them. He was a lonely man like his father, but not content with loneliness; friendship was always strong to tempt him, and when the thought of something more than friendship had been suffered to take hold upon his imagination, it held with terrible grip, burning, torturing. He had come simply to meet Cecily; there was the long and short of it. It was a weakness, such as any man may be guilty of, particularly any artist who groans in lifelong solitude. Let it be recognized; let it be flung savagely into the past, like so many others encountered and overcome on his course.

The other day, when it was rainy and sunless, he had seemed all at once to find his freedom. In a moment of mental languor, he was able to view his position clearly, as though some other man were concerned, and to cry out that he had triumphed; but within the same hour an event befell which revived all the old trouble and added new. Reuben Elgar entered his room, coming directly from Villa Sannazaro, in a state of excitement, talking at once of Cecily Doran as though his acquaintance with her had been unbroken from the time when she was in his mother's care to now. Irritation immediately scattered the thoughts Mallard had been ranging; he could barely make a show of amicable behaviour; a cold fear began to creep about his heart. The next morning he awoke to a new phase

of his conflict, the end further off than ever.
Unable to command thought and feeling, he
preserved at least the control of his action,
and could persevere in the resolve not to
see Cecily ; to avoid casual meetings he kept
away even from the Spences. He shunned
all places likely to be visited by Cecily, and
either sat at home in dull idleness or strayed
about the swarming quarters of the town,
trying to entertain himself with the spectacle
of Neapolitan life. To-day the delicious
weather had drawn him forth heedlessly.
And, indeed, it did not much matter now
whether he met his friends or not; he had
spoken the word—to-morrow he would go
his way.

At the very moment of thinking this
thought, when his cigar was nearly finished
and he had begun to stretch his limbs,
wearied by remaining in one position,
shadows and footsteps approached him. He
looked up, and——

" Mr. Mallard ! So we have caught you
at last ! It only needed this to complete

our enjoyment. Now you will go across to Baiæ with us."

Cecily, with Mrs. Baske and Spence. She had run eagerly forward, and her companions were advancing at a more sober pace. Mallard rose with his grim smile, and of course forgot that it is customary to doff one's beaver when ladies approach ; he took the offered hand, said "How do you do ?" and turned to the others.

"A fair capture !" exclaimed Spence. "Just now, at lunch, we were speculating on such a chance. The cigar argues a broken fast, I take it."

"Yes, I have had my maccheroni."

"We are going to take a boat over to Baiæ. Suppose you come with us."

"Of course Mr. Mallard will come," said Cecily, her face radiant. "He can make no pretence of work interrupted."

Already the group was surrounded by boatmen offering their services. Spence led the way down to the quay, and after much tumult a boat was selected and a bargain struck, the original demand made by the artless sailors being of course five times as much as was ever paid for the transit. They rowed out through the cluster of little craft, then hoisted a sail, and glided smoothly over the blue water.

" Where is Mrs. Lessingham ? " Mallard inquired of Cecily.

" At the Hôtel Bristol, with some very disagreeable people who have just landed on their way from India—a military gentleman, and a more military lady, and a most military son, relatives of ours. We spent last evening with them, and I implored to be let off to-day."

Mallard propped himself idly, and from under the shadow of his hat often looked at her. He had begun to wonder at the unreserved joy with which she greeted his joining the party. Of course she could have no slightest suspicion of what was in his mind ; one moment's thought of him in such a light must have altered her behaviour immediately. Altered in what way ? That

he in vain tried to imagine ; his knowledge
of her did not go far enough. But he could
not be wrong in attributing unconsciousness
to her. Moreover, with the inconsistency
of a man in his plight, he resented it. To
sit thus, almost touching him, gazing freely
into his face, and yet to be in complete
ignorance of suffering which racked him,
seemed incompatible with fine qualities
either of heart or mind. What rubbish
was talked about woman's insight, about
her delicate sympathies !

" Mrs. Spence is very sorry not to see
you occasionally, Mr. Mallard."

It was Miriam who spoke. Mallard was
watching Cecily, and now, on turning his
head, he felt sure that Mrs. Baske had been
observant of his countenance. Her eyes fell
whilst he was seeking words for a reply.

" I shall call to see her to-morrow morning," he said, " just to say good-bye for a
time."

" You really go to-morrow ? " asked Cecily,
with interest, but nothing more.

"Yes. I hope to see Mrs. Lessingham for a moment also. Can you tell me when she is likely to be at home?"

"Certainly between two and three, if you could come then."

He waited a little, then looked unexpectedly at Miriam. Again her eyes were fixed on him, and again they fell with something of consciousness. Did *she*, perchance, understand him?

His speculations concerning Cecily became comparative—the only hopeful method, we know, in whatsoever science. In point of age, the distance between Cecily and Miriam was of some importance; the fact that the elder had been a married woman was of still more account. On the first day of his meeting with Mrs. Baske, he had thought a good deal about her; since then she had slipped from his mind, but now he felt his interest reviving. Surely she was as remote from him as a woman well could be, yet his attitude towards her had no character of intolerance; he half wished that he could form

a closer acquaintance with her.   At present,
the thought of calm conversation with such
a woman made a soothing contrast to the
riot excited in him by Cecily.   Did she
read his mind ?   For one thing, it was not
impossible that the Spences had spoken
freely in her presence of himself and his odd
relations to the girl ; there was no doubting
how *they* regarded him.   Possibly he was
a frequent subject of discussion between
Eleanor and her cousin.   Mature women
could talk with each other freely of these
things.

On the other hand, whatever Mrs. Lessingham might have in her mind, she
certainly would not expose it in dialogue
with her niece.   Cecily was in an unusual
position for a girl of her age ; she had, he
believed, no intimate friend ; at all events,
she had none who also knew him.   Girls,
to be sure, had their own way of talking
over delicate points, just as married women
had theirs, and with intimates of the
ordinary kind Cecily must have come by

now to consider her guardian as a male creature of flesh and blood. What did it mean, that she did not?

A question difficult of debate, involving much that the mind is wont to slur over in natural scruple. Mallard was no slave to the imbecile convention which supposes a young girl sexless in her understanding; he could not, in conformity with the school of hypocritic idealism, regard Cecily as a child of woman's growth. No. She had the fruits of a modern education; she had a lucid brain; of late she had mingled and conversed with a variety of men and women, most of them anything but crassly conventional. It was this very aspect of her training that had caused him so much doubt. And he knew by this time what his doubt principally meant; in a measure, it came of native conscientiousness, of prejudice which testified to his origin; but, more than that, it signified simple jealousy. Secretly, he did not like her outlook upon the world to be so unrestrained; he would have preferred

her to view life as a simpler matter. Partly
for this reason did her letters so disturb
him. No; it would have been insult to
imagine her with the moral sensibilities of
a child of twelve.

Was she intellectual at the expense of
her emotional being? Was she guarded
by nature against these disturbances?
Somewhat ridiculous to ask that, and then
look up at her face effulgent with the joy
of life. She who could not speak without
the note of emotion, who so often gave way
to lyrical outbursts of delight, who was so
warm-hearted in her friendship, whose every
movement was in glad harmony with the
loveliness of her form,—must surely have
the corresponding capabilities of passion.

After all—and it was fetching a great compass to reach a point so near at hand—might
she not take him at his own profession?
Might she not view him as a man indeed,
and one not yet past his youth, but still as
a man who suffered no trivialities to interfere
with the grave objects of his genius? She

had so long had him represented to her in that way—from the very first of their meetings, indeed. Grant her mature sense and a reflective mind, was that any reason why she should probe subtly the natural appearance of her friend, and attribute to him that which he gave no sign of harbouring? Why must she be mysteriously conscious of his inner being, rather than take him ingenuously for what he seemed? She had instruction and wit, but she was only a girl; her experience was as good as *nil*. Mallard repeated that to himself as he looked at Mrs. Baske. To a great extent Cecily did, in fact, inhabit an ideal world. She was ready to accept the noble as the natural. Untroubled herself, she could contemplate without scepticism the image of an artist finding his bliss in solitary toil. This was the ground of the respect she had for him; disturb this idea, and he became to her quite another man—one less interesting, and, it might be, less lovable in either sense of the word.

Spence maintained a conversation with Miriam, chiefly referring to the characteristics of the scene about them; he ignored her peculiarities, and talked as though everything must necessarily give her pleasure. Her face proved that at all events the physical influences of this day in the open air were beneficial. The soft breeze had brought a touch of health to her cheek, and languid inattention no longer marked her gaze at sea and shore; she was often absent, but never listless. When she spoke, her voice was subdued and grave; it always caused Mallard to glance in her direction.

At Baiæ they dismissed the boat, purposing to drive back to Naples. In their ramble among the ruins, Mallard did his best to be at ease and seem to share Cecily's happiness; in any case, it was better to talk of the Romans than of personal concerns. When in after-time he recalled this day, it seemed to him that he had himself been well contented; it dwelt in his memory with a sunny glow. He saw Cecily's unsurpassable grace as she walked beside him, and her look of winning candour turned to him so often, and he fancied that it had given him pleasure to be with her. And pleasure there was, no doubt, but inextricably blended with complex miseries. To Cecily his mood appeared more gracious than she had ever known it; he did not disdain to converse on topics which presupposed some knowledge on her part, and there was something of unusual gentleness in his tone which she liked.

"Some day," she said, "we shall talk of Baiæ in London, in a November fog."

"I hope not."

"But such contrasts help one to get the most out of life," she rejoined, laughing. "At all events, when some one happens to speak to me of Mr. Mallard's pictures, I shall win credit by casually mentioning that I was at Baiæ in his company in such-and-such a year."

"You mean, when I have painted my last?"

"No, no! It would be no pleasure to me to anticipate that time."

"But natural, in talking with a veteran."

It was against his better purpose that he let fall these words; they contained almost a hint of his hidden self, and he had not yet allowed anything of the kind to escape him. But the moment proved too strong.

"A veteran who fortunately gives no sign of turning grey," replied Cecily, glancing at his hair.

An interruption from Spence put an end to this dangerous dialogue. Mallard, inwardly growling at himself, resisted the temptation to further *tête-à-tête*, and in a short time the party went in search of a conveyance for their return. None offered that would hold four persons; the ordinary public carriages have convenient room for two only, and a separation was necessary. Mallard succeeded in catching Spence's eye, and made him understand with a savage look that he was to take Cecily with him. This arrangement was effected, and the first

carriage drove off with those two, Cecily
exchanging merry words with an old Italian
who had rendered no kind of service, but
came to beg his *mancia* on the strength of
being able to utter a few sentences in
English.

For the first time, Mallard was alone with
Mrs. Baske. Miriam had not concealed
surprise at the new adjustment of companionship; she looked curiously both at
Cecily and at Mallard whilst it was going
on. The first remark which the artist
addressed to her, when they had been driving for a few minutes, was perhaps, she
thought, an explanation of the proceeding.

"I shall meet your brother again at
Pompeii to-morrow, Mrs. Baske."

"Have you seen much of him since he
came?" Miriam asked constrainedly. She
had not met Mallard since Reuben's arrival.

"Oh yes. We have dined together each
evening."

Between two such unloquacious persons,
dialogue was naturally slow at first, but

they had a long drive before them.　Miriam presently trusted herself to ask :

" Has he spoken to you at all of his plans —of what he is going to do when he returns to England ? "

" In general terms only.　He has literary projects."

" Do you put any faith in them, Mr. Mallard ? "

This was a sudden step towards intimacy. As she spoke, Miriam looked at him in a way that he felt to be appealing.　He answered the look frankly.

" I think he has the power to do something worth doing.　Whether his perseverance will carry him through it, is another question."

" He speaks to me of you in a way that—— He seems, I mean, to put a value on your friendship, and I think you may still influence him.　I am very glad he has met you here."

" I have very little faith in the influence of one person on another, Mrs. Baske.　For ill—yes, that is often seen ; but influence of the kind you suggest is the rarest of things."

"I'm afraid you are right."

She retreated into herself, and, when he looked at her, he saw cold reserve once more on her countenance.   Doubtless she did not choose to let him know how deeply this question of his power concerned her. Mallard felt something like compassion ; yet not ordinary compassion either, for at the same time he had a desire to break down this reserve, and see still more of what she felt.   Curious ; that evening when he dined at the villa, he had already become aware of this sort of attraction in her, an appeal to his sympathies together with the excitement of his combative spirit—if that expressed it.

"No man," he remarked, "ever did solid work except in his own strength.   One can be encouraged in effort, but the effort must originate in one's self."

Miriam kept silence.   He put a direct question.

"Have you yourself encouraged him to pursue this idea?"

"I have not *discouraged* him."

"In your brother's case, discouragement would probably be the result if direct encouragement were withheld."

Again she said nothing, and again Mallard felt a desire to subdue the pride, or whatever it might be, that had checked the growth of friendliness between them in its very beginning. He remained mute for a long time, until they were nearing Pozzuoli, but Miriam showed no disposition to be the first to speak. At length he said abruptly:

"Shall you go to the San Carlo during the winter?"

"The San Carlo?" she asked inquiringly.

"The opera."

Mallard was in a strange mood. Whenever he looked ahead at Cecily, he had a miserable longing which crushed his heart down, down; in struggling against this, he felt that Mrs. Baske's proximity was an aid, but that it would be still more so if he could move her to any unusual self-revelation. He had impulses to offend her, to irritate her prejudices—anything, so she should but be moved. This question that fell from him was mild in comparison with some of the subjects that pressed on his harassed brain.

"I don't go to theatres," Miriam replied distantly.

"That is losing much pleasure."

"The word has very different meanings."

She was roused. Mallard observed with a perverse satisfaction the scorn implied in this rejoinder. He noted that her features had more decided beauty than when placid.

"I imagine," he resumed, smiling at her, "that the life of an artist must seem to you frivolous, if not something worse. I mean an artist in the sense of a painter."

"I cannot think it the highest kind of life," Miriam replied, also smiling, but ominously.

"As Miss Doran does," added Mallard, his eyes happening to catch Cecily's face as it looked backwards, and his tongue speaking recklessly.

"There are very few subjects on which Miss Doran and I think alike."

He durst not pursue this; in his state of mind, the danger of committing some flagrant absurdity was too great. The subject attracted him like an evil temptation, for he desired to have Miriam speak of Cecily. But he mastered himself.

"The artist's life may be the highest of which a particular man is capable. For instance, I think it is so in my own case."

Miriam seemed about to keep silence again, but ultimately she spoke. The voice suggested that upon her too there was a constraint of some kind.

"On what grounds do you believe that?"

His eyes sought her face rapidly. Was she ironical at his expense? That would be new light upon her mind, for hitherto she had seemed to him painfully literal. Irony meant intellect; mere scorn or pride might signify anything but that. And he was hoping to find reserves of power in her, such as would rescue her from the imputation of commonplaceness in her beliefs. Testing her with his eye, he answered meaningly:

"Not, I admit, on the ground of recognized success."

Miriam made a nervous movement, and her brows contracted. Without looking at him, she said, in a voice which seemed rather to resent his interpretation than to be earnest in deprecating it:

"You know, Mr. Mallard, that I meant nothing of the kind."

"Yet I could have understood you, if you had. Naturally you must wonder a little at a man's passing his life as I do. You interpret life absolutely; it is your belief that it can have only one meaning, the same for all, involving certain duties of which there can be no question, and admitting certain relaxations which have endured the moral test. A man may not fritter away the years that are granted him; and that is what I seem to you to be doing, at best."

"Why should you suppose that I take upon myself to judge you?"

"Forgive me; I think it is one result of your mental habits that you judge all who differ from you."

This time she clearly was resolved to make no reply. They were passing through Pozzuoli, and she appeared to forget the discussion in looking about her. Mallard watched her, but she showed no consciousness of his gaze.

"Even if the world recognized me as an artist of distinction," he resumed, "you would still regard me as doubtfully employed. Art does not seem to you an end of sufficient gravity. Probably you had rather there were no such thing, if it were practicable."

"There is surely a great responsibility on any one who makes it the *end* of life."

This was milder again, and just when he had anticipated the opposite.

"A responsibility to himself, yes. Well, when I say that I believe this course is the highest I can follow, I mean that I believe it employs all my best natural powers as no other would. As for highest in the absolute sense, that is a different matter. Possibly the life of a hospital nurse, of a sister of mercy—something of that kind—comes nearest to the ideal."

She glanced at him, evidently in the same kind of doubt about his meaning as he had recently felt about hers.

"Why should you speak contemptuously of such people?"

"Contemptuously? I speak sincerely. In a world where pain is the most obvious fact, the task of mercy must surely take precedence of most others."

"I am surprised to hear you say this."

It was spoken in the tone most characteristic of her, that of a proud condescension.

"Why, Mrs. Baske?"

She hesitated a little, but made answer:

"I don't mean that I think you unfeeling, but your interests seem to be so far from such simple things."

"True."

Again a long silence. The carriage was descending the road from Pozzuoli; it approached the sea-shore, where the gentle breakers were beginning to be tinged with evening light. Cecily looked back and waved her hand.

"When you say that art is an end in itself," Miriam resumed abruptly, "you claim, I suppose, that it is a way of serving mankind?"

Mallard was learning the significance of her tones. In this instance, he knew that the words "serving mankind" were a contemptuous use of a phrase she had heard, a phrase which represented the philosophy alien to her own.

"Indeed, I claim nothing of the kind," he replied, laughing. "Art may, or may not, serve such a purpose; but be assured that the artist never thinks of his work in that way."

"You make no claim, then, even of usefulness?"

"Most decidedly, none. You little imagine

how distasteful the word is to me in such connection."

"Then how can you say you are employing your best natural powers?"

She had fallen to ingenuous surprise, and Mallard again laughed, partly at the simplicity of the question, partly because it pleased him to have brought her to such directness.

"Because," he answered, "this work gives me keener and more lasting pleasure than any other would. And I am not a man easily pleased with my own endeavours, Mrs. Baske. I work with little or no hope of ever satisfying myself—that is another thing. I have heard men speak of my kind of art as 'the noble pursuit of Truth,' and so on. I don't care for such phrases; they may mean something, but as a rule come of the very spirit so opposed to my own—that which feels it necessary to justify art by bombast. The one object I have in life is to paint a bit of the world just as I see it. I exhaust myself in vain toil; I shall never succeed ; but I am right to persevere, I am right to go on pleasing myself."

Miriam listened in astonishment.

"With such views, Mr. Mallard, it is fortunate that you happen to find pleasure in painting pictures."

"Which, at all events, do people no harm."

She turned upon him suddenly.

"Do you encourage my brother in believing that his duty in life is to please himself?"

"It has been my effort," he replied gravely.

"I don't understand you," Miriam said, in indignation.

"No, you do not. I mean to say that I believe your brother is not really pleased with the kind of life he has too long been leading; that to please himself he must begin serious work of some kind."

"That is playing with words, and on a subject ill-chosen for it."

"Mrs. Baske, do you seriously believe that Reuben Elgar can be made a man of steady purpose by considerations that have primary reference to any one or anything but himself?"

She made no answer.

"I am not depreciating him. The same will apply (if you are content to face the truth) to many a man whom you would esteem. I am sorry that I have lost your confidence, but that is better than to keep it by repeating idle formulas that the world's experience has outgrown."

Miriam pondered, then said quietly:

"We have different thoughts, Mr. Mallard, and speak different languages."

"But we know a little more of each other than we did. For my part, I feel it a gain."

During the rest of the drive they scarcely spoke at all; the few sentences exchanged were mere remarks upon the scenery. Both carriages drew up at the gate of the villa, where Miriam and Mallard alighted. Spence, rising, called to the latter.

"Will you accompany Miss Doran the rest of the way?"

"Certainly."

Mallard took his seat in the other carriage ; and, as it drove off, he looked back. Miriam was gazing after them.

Cecily was a little tired, and not much disposed to converse. Her companion being still less so, they reached the Mergellina without having broached any subject.

"It has been an unforgettable day," Cecily said, as they parted.

CHAPTER VI.

CAPTIVE TRAVELLERS.

HE had taken leave of the Spences and
Mrs. Baske, yet was not sure that he
should go. He had said good-bye to Mrs.
Lessingham and to Cecily herself, yet
made no haste to depart. It drew on to
evening, and he sat idly in his room in
Casa Rolandi, looking at his traps half
packed. Then of a sudden up he started.
" Imbecile! Insensate! I give you fifteen
minutes to be on your way to the station.
Miss the next train—and sink to the level
of common men!" Shirts, socks—straps,
locks; adieux, tips—horses, whips! Clatter
through the Piazzetta Mondragone; down
at break-neck speed to the Via Roma; across
the Piazza del Municipio; a good-bye to
the public scriveners sitting at their little

tables by the San Carlo; sharp round the
corner, and along by the Porto Grande with
its throng of vessels. All the time he sings
a tune to himself, caught up in the streets
of the tuneful city; a lilting air. He does
not know the words; a pity, for the refrain
ran—

"Io ti voglio bene assaje
E tu non pienz' a me!"

Just after nightfall, he alighted from the
train at Pompeii. Having stowed away
certain impedimenta at the station, he took
his travelling-bag in his hand, broke with
small ceremony through porters and hotel-
touts, came forth upon the high-road, and
stepped forward like one to whom the
locality is familiar. In a minute or two he
was overtaken by a little lad, who looked
up at him and said in an insinuating voice,
"Albergo del Sole, signore?"

"Prendi, bambino," was Mallard's reply,
as he handed the bag to him. "Avanti!"

A divine evening, softly warm, dim-
glimmering. The dusty road ran on between

white trunks of plane-trees; when the station and the houses near it were left behind, no other building came in view. To the left of the road, hidden behind its long earth-rampart, lay the dead city; far beyond rose the dark shape of Vesuvius, crested with beacon-glow, a small red fire, now angry, now murky, now for a time extinguished. The long rumble of the train died away, and there followed silence absolute, scarcely broken for a few minutes by a peasant singing in the distance, the wailing song so often heard in the south of Italy. Silence that was something more than the wonted soundlessness of night; the haunting oblivion of a time long past, a melancholy brooding voiceless upon the desolate home of forgotten generations.

A walk of ten minutes, and there shone light from windows. The lad ran forward and turned in at the gate of a garden; Mallard followed, and approached some persons who were standing at an open door. He speedily made arrangements for his night's lodging, saw his room, and went to the quarter of the inn where dinner was already in progress. This was a building to itself, at one side of the garden. Through the doorway he stepped immediately into a low-roofed hall, where a number of persons sat at table. Pillars supported the ceiling in the middle, and the walls were in several places painted with heads or landscapes, the work of artists who had made their abode here; one or two cases with glass doors showed relics of Pompeii.

Elgar was one of the company. When he became aware of Mallard's arrival, he stood up with a cry of "All hail!" and pointed to a seat near him.

"I began to be afraid you wouldn't come this evening. Try the risotto; it's excellent. Ye gods! what an appetite I had when I sat down! To-day have I ascended Vesuvius. How many bottles of wine I drank between starting and returning I cannot compute; I never knew before what it was to be athirst. Why, their vino di

Vesuvio is for all the world like cider; I thought at first I was being swindled—not an impossible thing in these regions. I must tell you a story about a party of Americans I encountered at Bosco Reale."

The guests numbered seven or eight; with one exception besides Elgar, they were Germans, all artists of one kind or another, fellows of genial appearance, loud in vivacious talk. The exception was a young Englishman, somewhat oddly dressed, and with a great quantity of auburn hair that rolled forward upon his distinguished brow. At a certain *pension* on the Mergellina he was well known. He sat opposite Elgar, and had been in conversation with him.

Mallard cared little what he ate, and ate little of anything. Neither was he in the mood for talk; but Elgar, who had finished his solid meal, and now amused himself with grapes (in two forms), spared him the necessity of anything but an occasional monosyllable. The young man was elated, and grew more so as he proceeded with his dessert; his cheeks were deeply flushed; his eyes gleamed magnificently.

In the mean time, Clifford Marsh had joined in conversation with the Germans; his use of their tongue was far from idiomatic, but by sheer determination to force a way through linguistic obstacles, he talked with a haphazard fluency which was amusing enough. No false modesty imposed a check upon his eloquence. It was to the general table that he addressed himself on the topic that had arisen; in an English dress his speech ran somewhat as follows :—

"Gentlemen, allow me to say that I have absolutely no faith in the future of which you speak! It is my opinion that democracy is the fatal enemy of art. How can you speak of ancient and mediæval states? Neither in Greece nor in Italy was there ever what we understand by a democracy."

"Factisch! Der Herr hat Recht!" cried some one, and several other voices strove to make themselves heard; but the orator raised his note and overbore interruption.

" You must excuse me, gentlemen, if I say that—however it may be from other points of view—from the standpoint of art, democracy is simply the triumph of ignorance and brutality." ("Gewisz!"—"Nimmermehr!"—"Vortrefllich!") "I don't care to draw distinctions between forms of the thing. Socialism, communism, collectivism, parliamentarism,—all these have one and the same end: to put men on an equality; and in proportion as that end is approached, so will art in every shape languish. Art, gentlemen, is nourished upon inequalities and injustices!" ("Ach!"—"Wie kann man so etwas sagen!"—"Hoch! verissime!") "I am not representing this as either good or bad. It may be well that justice should be established, even though art perish. I simply state a fact!" ("Doch!" — "Erlauben Sie!") "Supremacy of the vulgar interest means supremacy of ignoble judgment in all matters of mind. See what plutocracy already makes of art!"

Here one of the Germans insisted on a hearing; a fine fellow, with Samsonic locks and a ringing voice.

" Sir! sir! who talks of a genuine democracy with mankind in its present state? Before it comes about, the multitude will be instructed, exalted, emancipated, humanized!"

"Sir!" shouted Marsh, "who talks of the Millennium? I speak of things possible within a few hundred years. The multitude will *never* be humanized. Civilization is attainable only by the few; nature so ordains it."

"Pardon me for saying that is a lie! I use the word controversially."

"It is a manifest truth!" cried the other. "Who ever doubted it but a *Dummkopf?* I use the word with reference to this argument only."

So it went on for a long time. Mallard and Elgar knew no German, so could derive neither pleasure nor profit from the high debate.

" Are you as glum here as in London ? "
Reuben asked of his companion, in a banter-
ing voice. " I should have pictured you
grandly jovial, wreathed perhaps with ruddy
vine-leaves, the light of inspiration in your
eye, and in your hand a mantling goblet !
Drink, man, drink ! you need a stimulant,
an exhilarant, an anti-phlegmatic, a counter-
irritant against English spleen. You are
still on the other side of the Alps, of the
Channel ; the fogs yet cling about you.
Clear your brow, O painter of Ossianic
wildernesses ! Taste the foam of life ! We
are in the land of Horace, and *nunc est
bibendum !* Seriously, do you *never* relax ? "

" Oh yes. You should see me over the
fifth tumbler of whiskey at Stornoway."

" Bah ! you might as well say the fifth
draught of fish-oil at the North Cape. How
innocent this wine is ! A gallon of it would
give one no more than a pleasant glow,
the faculty of genial speech. Take a glass
with me to the health of your enchanting
ward."

"Please to command your tongue," growled Mallard, with a look that was not to be mistaken.

"I beg your pardon. It shall be to the health of that superb girl we saw in the Mercato. But, as far as I can judge yet, the Neapolitan type doesn't appeal to me very strongly. It is finely animal, and of course that has its value; but I prefer the suggestion of a soul, don't you? I remember a model old Langton had in Rome, a girl fresh from the mountains; by Juno! a glorious creature? I dare say you have seen her portrait in his studio; he likes to show it. But it does her nothing like justice; she might have sat for the genius of the Republic. Utterly untaught, and intensely stupid; but there were marvellous things to be read into her face. Ah, but give me the girls of Venice! You know them, how they walk about the Piazza; their tall, lithe forms, the counterpart of the gondolier; their splendid black hair, elaborately braided and pierced with large ornaments; their noble, aristocratic, grave features; their long shawls! What natural dignity! What eloquent eyes! I like to imagine them profoundly intellectual, which they are unhappily not."

Marsh had withdrawn from colloquy with the Germans, and kept glancing across the table at his compatriots, obviously wishing that he might join them. Mallard, upon whom Elgar's excited talk jarred more and more, noticed the stranger's looks, and at length leaned forward to speak to him.

"As usual, we are in a minority among the sun-worshippers."

"Sun-worshippers! Good!" laughed the other. "Yes, I have never met more than one or two chance Englishmen at the 'Sole.'"

"But you are at your ease with our friends there.—I think you know as little German as I do, Elgar?"

"Devilish bad at languages! To tell you the truth, I can't endure the sense of inferiority one has in beginning to smatter with foreigners. I read four or five, but avoid speaking as much as possible."

Marsh took an early opportunity of alluding to the argument in which he had recently taken part. The subject was resumed. At Elgar's bidding the waiter had brought cigars, and things looked comfortable ; the Germans talked with more animation than ever.

" One of the worst evils of democracy in England," said Reuben, forcibly, " is its alliance with Puritan morality."

" Oh, that is being quickly outgrown," cried Marsh. " Look at the spread of rationalism."

" You take it for granted that Puritanism doesn't survive religious dogma ? Believe me, you are greatly mistaken. I am sorry to say I have a large experience in this question. The mass of the English people have no genuine religious belief, but none the less they are Puritans in morality. The same applies to the vastly greater part of those who even repudiate Christianity."

"One must take account of the national hypocrisy," remarked the younger man, with an air of superiority, shaking his head as his habit was.

"It's a complicated matter. The representative English bourgeois is a hypocrite in essence, but is perfectly serious in his judgment of the man next door; and the latter characteristic has more weight than the former in determining his life. Puritanism has aided the material progress of England; but its effect on art! But for it, we should have a school of painters corresponding in greatness to the Elizabethan dramatists. Depend upon it, the democracy will continue to be Puritan. Every picture, every book, will be tried by the same imbecile test. Enforcement of Puritan morality will be one of the ways in which the mob, come to power, will revenge itself on those who still remain its superiors."

Marsh was not altogether pleased at finding his facile eloquence outdone. In comparing himself with Elgar, he was conscious of but weakly representing the tendencies which were a passionate force in this man with the singularly fine head, with such a glow of wild life about him. He abandoned the abstract argument, and struck a personal note.

"However it may be in the future, I grant you the artist has at present no scope save in one direction. For my own part, I have fallen back on landscape. Let those who will, paint Miss Wilhelmina in the nursery, with an interesting doll of her own size; or a member of Parliament rising to deliver a great speech on the liquor traffic; or Mrs. What-do-you-call-her, lecturing on woman's rights. These are the subjects our time affords."

Mallard eyed with fresh curiosity the gentleman who had "fallen back on landscape."

"What did you formerly aim at?" he inquired, with a sort of suave gruffness.

"Things which were hopelessly out of the question. I worked for a long time at a

'Death of Messalina.' That was in Rome.
I had a splendid inspiration for Messalina's
face. But my hand was paralyzed when I
thought of the idiotic comments such a
picture would occasion in England. One
fellow would say I had searched through
history in a prurient spirit for something
sensational; another, that I read a moral
lesson of terrible significance; and so on."

"A grand subject, decidedly!" exclaimed
Elgar, with genuine enthusiasm, which re-
stored Marsh to his own good opinion.
"Go on with it! Bid the fools be hanged!
Have you your studies here?"

"Unfortunately not. They are in Rome."

Mallard delivered himself of a blunt
opinion.

"That is no subject for a picture. Use it
for literature, if you like."

The inevitable discussion began, the discussion so familiar nowadays, and which
would have sounded so odd to the English
painters who were wont to call themselves
"historical." Where is the line between

subjects for the easel and subjects for the desk? What distinguishes the art of the illustrator from the art of the artist?

That was a great evening round the table at the Albergo del Sole. How gloriously the air thickened with tobacco-smoke! What removal of empty bottles and re-placing them with full! The Germans were making it a set *Kneipe;* the Englishmen, unable to drink quite so heroically, were scarce behind in vehemence of debate. Mallard, grimly accepting the help of wine against his inner foes, at length earned Elgar's approval; he had relaxed indeed, and was no longer under the oppression of English fog. But with him such moods were of brief duration; he suddenly quitted the table, and went out into the night air.

The late moon was rising, amber-coloured on a sky of dusky azure. He walked from the garden, across the road, and towards the ruins of the Amphitheatre, which lie some distance apart from the Pompeian streets that have been unearthed; he passed beneath an arch, and stood looking down into the dark hollow so often thronged with citizens of Latin speech. Small wonder that Benvenuto's necromancer could evoke his myriads of flitting ghosts in the midnight Colosseum ; here too it needed but to stand for a few minutes in the dead stillness, and the air grew alive with mysterious presences, murmurous with awful whisperings. Mallard enjoyed it for a while, but at length turned away abruptly, feeling as if a cold hand had touched him.

As he re-entered the inn-precincts, he heard voices still uproarious in the dining-room ; but he had no intention of going among them again. His bedroom was one of a row each of which opened immediately upon the garden. He locked himself in, went to bed, but did not sleep for a long time. A wind was rising, and a branch of a tree constantly tapped against the pane. It might have been some centuries-dead inhabitant of Pompeii trying to deliver a message from the silent world.

The breakfast-party next morning lacked vivacity. Clifford Marsh was mute and dolorous of aspect ; no doubt his personal embarrassments were occupying him. Yesterday's wine had become his foe, instead of an ally urging him to dare all in the cause of "art." He consumed his coffee and roll in the manner of ordinary mortals, not once flourishing his dainty hand or shaking his ambrosial hair. Elgar was very stiff from his ascent of Vesuvius, and he too found that "the foam of life" had an unpleasant after-taste, suggestive of wrecked fortunes and a dubious future. Mallard was only a little gruffer than his wonted self.

"I am going on at once to Sorrento," he said, meeting Elgar afterwards in the garden. "To-morrow I shall cross over the hills to Positano and Amalfi. Suppose you come with me ?"

The other hesitated.

"You mean you are going to walk ?"

"No. I have traps to carry on from the station. We should have a carriage to

Sorrento, and to-morrow a donkey for the baggage."

They paced about, hands in pockets. It was a keen morning; the tramontana blew blusterously, causing the smoke of Vesuvius to lie all down its long slope, a dense white cloud, or a vast turbid torrent, breaking at the foot into foam and spray. The clearness of the air was marvellous. Distance seemed to have no power to dim the details of the landscape. The Apennines glistened with new-fallen snow.

"I hadn't thought of going any further just now," said Elgar, who seemed to have a difficulty in simply declining the invitation, as he wished to do.

"What should you do, then?"

"Spend another day here, I think,—I've only had a few hours among the ruins, you know,—and then go back to Naples."

"What to do there?" asked Mallard, bluntly.

"Give a little more time to the museum, and see more of the surroundings."

"Better come on with me. I shall be glad of your company."

It was said with decision, but scarcely with heartiness. Elgar looked about him vaguely.

"To tell you the truth," he said at last, "I don't care to incur much expense."

"The expenses of what I propose are trivial."

"My traps are at Naples, and I have kept the room there. No, I don't see my way to it, Mallard."

"All right."

The artist turned away. He walked about the road for ten minutes.—Very well; then he too would return to Naples. Why? What was altered? Even if Elgar accompanied him to Amalfi, it would only be for a few days; there was no preventing the fellow's eventual return—his visits to the villa, perhaps to Madame Glück's. Again imbecile and insensate! What did it all matter?

He stopped short. He would sit down

and write a letter to Mrs. Baske.—A pretty complication, that! What grounds for such a letter as he meditated?

The devil! Had he not a stronger will than Reuben Elgar? If he wished to carry a point with such a weakling, was he going to let himself be thwarted? Grant it was help only for a few days, no matter; Elgar should go with him.

He walked back to the garden. Good; there the fellow loitered, obviously irresolute.

"Elgar, you'd better come, after all," he said, with a grim smile. "I want to have some talk with you. Let us pay our shot, and walk on to the station."

"What kind of talk, Mallard?"

"Various. Get whatever you have to carry; I'll see to the bill."

"But how can I go on without a shirt?"

"I have shirts in abundance. A truce to your obstacles. March!"

And before very long they were side by side in the vehicle, speeding along the level road towards Castellammare and the mountains. This exertion of native energy had been beneficial to Mallard's temper; he talked almost genially. Elgar, too, had subdued his restiveness, and began to look forward with pleasure to the expedition.

"I only wish this wind would fall!" he exclaimed. "It's cold, and I hate a wind of any kind."

"Hate a wind? You're effeminate; you're a boulevardier. It would do you good to be pitched in a gale about the coast of Skye. A fellow of your temperament has no business in these relaxing latitudes. You want tonics."

"Too true, old man. I know myself at least as well as you know me."

"Then what a contemptible creature you must be! If a man knows his weakness, he is inexcusable for not overcoming it."

"A preposterous contradiction, allow me to say. A man is what he is, and will be ever the same. Have you no tincture of philosophy? You talk as though one could govern fate."

"And you, very much like the braying jackass in the field there."

Mallard had a savage satisfaction in breaking all bounds of civility. He overwhelmed his companion with abuse, revelled in insulting comparisons. Elgar laughed, and stretched himself on the cushions so as to avoid the wind as much as possible.

They clattered through the streets of Castellammare, pursued by urchins, crying, "Un sordo, signori!" Thence on by the seaside road to Vico Equense, Elgar every now and then shouting his ecstasy at the view. The hills on this side of the promontory climb, for the most part, softly and slowly upwards, everywhere thickly clad with olives and orange-trees, fig-trees and aloes. Beyond Vico comes a jutting headland; the road curves round it, clinging close on the hillside, turns inland, and all at once looks down upon the Piano di Sorrento. Instinctively, the companions rose to their feet, as though any other attitude on the first revelation of such a prospect were irreverent. It is not really a plain, but a gently rising wide and deep lap, surrounded by lofty mountains and ending at a line of sheer cliffs along the sea-front. A vast garden planted for Nature's joy; a pleasance of the gods; a haunt of the spirit of beauty set between sun-smitten crags and the enchanted shore.

"Heaven be praised that you forced me to come!" muttered Elgar, in his choking throat.

Mallard could say nothing. He had looked upon this scene before, but it affected him none the less.

They drove into the town of Tasso, and to an inn which stood upon the edge of a profound gorge, cloven towards the sea-cliffs. Sauntering in the yard whilst dinner was made ready, they read an inscription on a homely fountain:

"Sordibus abstersis, instructo marmore, priscus
Fons nitet, et manat gratior unda tibi."

"Eternal gratitude to our old school-masters," cried Elgar, "who thrashed us

through the Eton Latin grammar! What
is Italy to the man who cannot share our
feelings as we murmur that distich? I
marvel that I was allowed to learn this
heathen tongue. Had my parents known
what it would mean to me, I should never
have chanted my *hic, hæc, hoc*."

He was at his best this afternoon; Mallard could scarcely identify him with the
reckless, and sometimes vulgar, spendthrift
who had been rushing his way to ruin in
London. His talk abounded in quotation,
in literary allusion, in high-spirited jest, in
poetical feeling. When had he read so
much? What a memory he had! In a
world that consisted of but one sex, what
a fine fellow he would have been!

"What do you think of my sister?" he
asked, *à propos* of nothing, as they idled
about the Capo di Sorrento and on the road
to Massa.

"An absurd question."

"You mean that I cannot suppose you
would tell me the truth."

"And just as little the untruth. I do not know your sister."

"We had a horrible scene that day I turned up. I behaved brutally to her, poor girl."

"I'm afraid you have often done so."

"Often. I rave at her superstition ; how can she help it ? But she's a good girl, and has wit enough if she might use it. Oh, if some generous, large-brained man would drag her out of that slough of despond !—What a marriage that was ! Powers of darkness, what a marriage ! "

Mallard was led to no question.

"I shall never understand it, never,' went on Elgar, in excitement. "If you had seen that oily beast ! I don't know what criterion girls have. Several of my acquaintance have made marriages that set my hair on end. Lives thrown away in accursed ignorance—that's my belief."

Mallard waited for the next words, expecting that they would torture him. There was a long pause, however, and what he awaited did not come.

"Do you hate the name Miriam, as I do?"

"Hate it, no."

"I wonder they didn't call her Keziah, and me Mephibosheth. It isn't a nice thing to detest the memory of one's parents, Mallard. It doesn't help to make one a well-balanced man. How on earth did I get my individuality? And you mustn't think that Miriam is just what she seems—I mean, there *are* possibilities in her; I am convinced of it."

"Did it ever occur to you that your own proceedings may have acted as a check upon those possibilities?"

"I don't know that I ever thought of it," said Elgar, ingenuously.

"You never reflected that her notion of the liberated man is yourself?"

"You are right, Mallard. I see it. What other example had she?"

They walked as far as Massa Lubrense, a little town on the steep shore; over against it the giant cliffs of Capri, every cleft and scar and jutting rock discernible through the pellucid air, every minutest ruggedness casting its clear-cut shadow. But the surpassing glory was the prospect at the Cape of Sorrento when they reached it on their walk back. Before them the entire sweep of the gulf, from Ischia to Capri; Naples in its utmost extent, an unbroken line of delicate pink, from Posilipo to Torre Annunziata. Far below their feet the little *marina* of Sorrento, with its row of boats drawn up on the strand; behind them noble limestone heights. The sea was foaming under the tramontana, and its foam took colour from the declining sun.

Next morning they set forth again as Mallard had proposed, their baggage packed on a donkey, a guide with them to lead the way over the mountains to the other shore. A long climb, and at the culminating point of the ridge they rested to look the last on Naples; thenceforward their faces were set to the far blue hills of Calabria.

"Yonder lies Pæstum," said Mallard, pointing to the dim plain beyond the Gulf of Salerno; and his companion's eyes were agleam.

Early in the afternoon they reached the coast at Positano, and thence took boat for Amalfi. Elgar was like one possessed at his first sight of the wonderful old town, nested in its mountain gorge, overlooked by wild crags; this relic saved from the waste of mediæval glory. When they had put up at the Albergo d'Italia, he would not rest until he had used the last hour of sunlight in clambering about the little maze of streets, or rather of mountain paths and burrows beneath houses piled one upon another indistinguishably. Forced back by hunger, he still lingered upon the window-balcony, looking up at the hoary riven tower set high above the town on what seems an inaccessible peak, or at the cathedral and its many-coloured campanile.

How could Mallard help comparing these manifestations of ardent temper with what he had witnessed in Cecily? The resemblance was at moments more than he could endure; once or twice he astonished Elgar with a reply of unprovoked savageness. The emotions of the day, even more than its bodily exercise, had so wearied him that he went early to bed. They had a double-bedded room, and Elgar continued talking for hours. Even without this, Mallard felt that he would have been unable to sleep. To add to his torments, the clock of the cathedral, which was just on the opposite side of the street, had the terrible southern habit of striking the whole hour after the chime at each quarter; by midnight the clangour was all but incessant. Elgar sank at length into oblivion, but to his companion sleep came not. Very early in the morning there sounded the loud blast of a horn, all through the town and away into remoteness. Signify what it might, the practical result seemed to be a rousing of the population to their daily life; lively voices, the tramp of feet, the clatter of vehicles began at once, and waxed with the spread of day-light.

The sun rose, but only to gleam for an hour on clouds and vapours which it had not power to disperse. The mountain summits were hidden, and down their sides crept ominously the ragged edges of mist; a thin rain began to fall, and grew heavier as the sky dulled. Having breakfasted, the two friends spent an hour in the Cathedral, which was dark and chill and gloomy. Two or three old people knelt in prayer, their heads bowed against column or wall; re-marking the strangers, they came up to them and begged.

"My spirits are disagreeably on the ebb," said Elgar. "If it's to be a Scotch day, let us do some mountaineering."

They struck up the gorge, intending to pursue the little river, but were soon lost among ascents and descents, narrow stairs, precipitous gardens, and noisy paper-mills. Probably no unassisted mortal ever made his way out of Amalfi into the mountain slopes. They had scorned to take a guide, but did so at length in self-defence, so pestered were they by all but every person they passed; man, woman, and child beset them for soldi, either frankly begging or offering a direction and then extending their hands. The paper-mills were not romantic; the old women who came along bending under huge bales of rags were anything but picturesque. And it rained, it rained.

Wet and weary, they had no choice but to return to the inn. Elgar's animation had given place to fretfulness; Mallard, after his miserable night, cared little to converse, and would gladly have been alone. A midday meal, with liberal supply of wine, helped them somewhat, and they sat down to smoke in their bedroom. It rained harder than ever; from the window they could see the old tower on the crag smitten with white scud.

"Come now," said Mallard, forcing himself to take a livelier tone, "tell me about those projects of yours. Are you serious in your idea of writing?"

"Perfectly serious."

"And what are you going to write?"

"That I haven't quite determined. I am revolving things. I have ideas without number."

"Too many for use, then. You need to live in some such place as this for a few weeks, and clear your thoughts. 'Company, villanous company,' is the first thing to be avoided."

"No doubt you are right."

But it was half-heartedly said, and with a restless glance towards the window. Mallard, in whose heart a sick weariness conflicted with his will and his desire, went on in a dogged way.

"I want to work here for a time." Work! The syllable was like lead upon his tongue, and the thought a desolation in his mind. "Write to your sister; get her to send your belongings from Casa Rolandi, together with a ream of scribbling-paper.

I shall be out of doors most of· the day, and no one will disturb you here. Use the opportunity, like a man. Fall to. I have a strong suspicion that it is now or never with you."

" I doubt whether I could do anything here."

" Perhaps not on a day like this ; but it is happily exceptional. Remember yesterday. Were I a penman, the view from this window in sunlight would make the ink flow nobly."

Elgar was mute for a few minutes.

" I believe I need a big town. Scenes like this dispose me to idle enjoyment. I have thought of settling in Paris for the next six months."

Mallard made a movement of irritation.

" Then why did you come here at all ? You say you have no money to waste."

" Oh, it isn't quite so bad with me as all that," replied Elgar, as if he slightly resented this interference with his private affairs.

Yet he had yesterday, in the flow of his good-humour, all but confessed that it was high time he looked out for an income. Mallard examined him askance. The other, aware of this scrutiny, put on a smile, and said with an air of self-conquest :

"But you are right ; I have every reason to trust your advice. I'll tell you what, Mallard. To-morrow I'll drive to Salerno, take the train to Naples, pack my traps, and relieve Miriam's mind by an assurance that I'm going to work in your company ; then at once come back here."

"I don't see the need of going to Naples. Write a letter. Here's paper ; here's pen and ink."

Elgar was again mute. His companion, in an access of intolerable suffering, cried out vehemently :

"Can't you see into yourself far enough to know that you are paltering with necessity ? Are you such a feeble creature that you must be at the mercy of every childish whim, and ruin yourself for lack of courage to do what you know you ought to do? If instability of nature had made such work of me as it has of you, I'd cut my throat just to prove that I could at least once make my hand obey my will!"

"It would be but the final proof of weakness," replied Elgar, laughing. "Or, to be more serious, what would it prove either one way or the other? If you cut your throat, it was your destiny to do so; just as it was to commit the follies that led you there. What is all this nonsense about weak men and strong men? I act as I am bound to act; I refrain as I am bound to refrain. You know it well enough."

This repeated expression of fatalism was genuine enough. It manifested a habit of his thought. One of the characteristics of our time is that it produces men who are determinists by instinct; who, anything but profound students or subtle reasoners, catch at the floating phrases of philosophy and recognize them as the index of their being, adopt them thenceforth as clarifiers of their vague self-consciousness. In certain moods, Elgar could not change from one seat to another without its being brought to his mind that he had moved by necessity. Such men live very near to the borders of madness. Be their conviction founded or not, their supreme danger is the ever-present possibility of its becoming a " fixed idea."

" What if that be true?" said Mallard, with unexpected coldness. " In practice we live as though our will were free. Otherwise, why discuss anything?"

" True. This very discussion is a part of the scheme of things, the necessary antecedent of something or other in your life and mine. I shall go to Naples to-morrow; I shall spend one day there; on the day after, I shall be with you again. My hand upon it, Mallard. I promise!"

He did so with energy. And for the moment Mallard was the truer fatalist.

Again they left the inn, this time going sea-ward. Still in rain, they walked towards Minori, along the road which is cut in the mountain-side, high above the beach. They talked about the massive strongholds which stand as monuments of the time when the coast-towns were in fear of pirates. Melancholy brooded upon land and sea; the hills of Calabria, yesterday so blue and clear, had vanished like a sunny hope.

The morrow revealed them again. But again for Mallard there had passed a night of much misery. On rising, he durst not speak, so bitter was he made by Elgar's singing and whistling. Yet he would not have cared to prevent the journey to Naples, had it been in his power. He was sick of Elgar's company; he wished for solitude. When his eyes fell on the materials of his art, he turned away in disgust.

"You'll get to work as soon as I'm gone," cried Reuben, cheerfully.

"Yes."

He said it to avoid conversation.

"Cheer up, old man! I shall not disappoint you this time. You have my promise."

" Yes."

A two-horsed carriage was at the door.
Mallard looked at it from the balcony,
and was direly tempted. No fear of his
yielding, however. It was not *his* fate to
scamper whither desire pointed him.

" I have already begun to work out an
idea," said Elgar, as he breakfasted merrily.
" I woke in the night, and it came to me as
I heard the bell striking. My mind is
always active when I am travelling ; ten to
one I shall come back ready to begin to
write. I fear there's no decent ink pur-
chasable in Amalfi ; I mustn't forget that.
By-the-by, is there anything I can bring
you ? "

" Nothing, thanks."

They went down together, shook hands,
and away drove the carriage. At the public
fountain in the little piazza, where stands
the image of Sant' Andrea, a group of
women were busy or idling, washing clothes
and vegetables and fish, drawing water in
vessels of beautiful shape, chattering in-

cessantly—such a group as may have gathered there any morning for hundreds of years. Children darted after the vehicle, with their perpetual cry of "Un sord', signor!" and Elgar royally threw to them a handful of coppers, looking back to laugh as they scrambled.

A morning of mornings, deliciously fresh after the rain, the air exquisitely fragrant. On the mountain-tops ever so slight a mist still clinging, moment by moment fading against the blue.

"Yes, I shall be able to work here," said Elgar within himself. "December, January, February; I can be ready with something for the spring."

CHAPTER VII.

THE MARTYR.

CLIFFORD Marsh left Pompeii on the same day as his two chance acquaintances; he returned to his quarters on the Mergellina, much perturbed in mind, beset with many doubts, with divers temptations. "Shall I the spigot wield?" Must the ambitions of his glowing youth come to naught, and he descend to rank among the Philistines? For, to give him credit for a certain amount of good sense, he never gravely contemplated facing the world in the sole strength of his genius. He knew one or two who had done so; before his mind's eye was a certain little garret in Chelsea, where an acquaintance of his, a man of real and various powers, was year after year taxing his brain and heart in a bitter struggle with penury; and these

glimpses of Bohemia were far from inspiring
Clifford with zeal for naturalization. Elated
with wine and companionship, he liked to
pose as one who was sacrificing "prospects"
to artistic conscientiousness; but, even
though he had "fallen back" on landscape,
he was very widely awake to the fact that
his impressionist studies would not supply
him with bread, to say nothing of butter—
and Clifford must needs have both.

That step-father of his was a well-to-
do manufacturer of shoddy in Leeds, one
Hibbert, a good-natured man on the whole,
but of limited horizon. He had married a
widow distinctly above his own social standing, and for a long time was content to
supply her idolized son with the means of
pursuing artistic studies in London and
abroad. But Mr. Hibbert had a strong
opinion that this money should by now
have begun to make some show of produc-
tiveness. Domestic grounds of dissatisfac-
tion ripened his resolve to be firm with
young Mr. Marsh. Mrs. Hibbert was

extravagant; doubtless her son was playing the fool in the same direction. After all, one could pay too much for the privilege of being snubbed by one's superior wife and step-son. If Clifford were willing to "buckle to" at sober business (it was now too late for him to learn a profession), well and good; he should have an opening at which many a young fellow would jump. Otherwise, let the fastidious gentleman pay his own tailor's bills.

Clifford's difficulties were complicated by his relations with Madeline Denyer. It was now a year since he had met Madeline at Naples, had promptly fallen in love with her face and her advanced opinions, and had won her affection in return. Frankness as to his circumstances was inevitable, and we know what had been the result. Clifford was then firm in the belief that, if he actually married, Mr. Hibbert would not have the heart to stop his allowance; Mrs. Denyer had reasons for thinking otherwise, and her daughter saw the case in the same light. It must be added, for the complete understanding of our artistic friend, that he presumed the Denyers to be better off than they really were; in fact, he was to a great extent misled. His dignity, if the worst came about, would not have shrunk from moderate assistance at the hands of his parents-in-law. Madeline knew well enough that nothing of this kind was possible, and in the end made her lover's mind clear on the point. Since then the course of these young people's affections had been anything but smooth. However, the fact remained that there *was* mutual affection—which, to be sure, made the matter worse.

Distinctly so since the estrangement which had followed Marsh's arrival at the boarding-house. He did not take Madeline's advice to seek another abode, and for two or three days Madeline knew not whether to be glad or offended at his remaining. For two or three days only; then she began to have a pronounced opinion on the subject. It was monstrous that he should stay under this roof and sit at this table, after what had happened. He had no delicacy ; he was behaving as no gentleman could. It was high time that her mother spoke to him.

Mrs. Denyer solemnly invited the young man to a private interview.

" Mr. Marsh," she began, with pained dignity, whilst Clifford stood before her twiddling his watch-chain, " I really think the time has come for me to ask an explanation of what is going on. My daughter distresses me by saying that all is at an end between you. If that is really the case, why do you continue to live here, when you must know how disagreeable it is to Madeline ? "

" Mrs. Denyer," replied Clifford, in a friendly tone, " there has been a misunderstanding between us, but I am very far from reconciling myself to the thought that everything is at an end. My remaining surely proves that."

" I should have thought so. But in that case I am obliged to ask you another question. What can you mean by paying undisguised attentions to another young lady who is living here ? "

" You astonish me. What foundation is there for such a charge ? "

" At least you won't affect ignorance as to the person of whom I speak. I assure you that I am not the only one who has noticed this."

" You misinterpret my behaviour altogether. Of course, you are speaking of Miss Doran. If your observation had been accurate, you would have noticed that Miss Doran gives me no opportunity of paying her attentions, if I wished. Certainly I have had conversations with Mrs. Lessingham, but I see no reason why I should deny myself that pleasure."

" This is sophistry. You walked about the museum with *both* these ladies for a long time yesterday."

Clifford was startled, and could not conceal it.

" Of course," he exclaimed, " if my movements are watched, with a view to my accusation—— ! "

And he broke off significantly, shaking his hair back.

"Your movements are not watched. But if I happen to hear of such things, I must draw my own conclusions."

"I give you my assurance that the meeting was purely by chance, and that our conversation was solely of indifferent matters —of art, of Pompeii, and so on."

"Perhaps you are not aware," resumed Mrs. Denyer, with a smile that made caustic comment on this apology, "that, when we sit at table, your eyes are directed to Miss Doran with a frequency that no one can help observing."

Marsh hesitated; then, throwing his head back, remarked in an unapproachable manner:

"Mrs. Denyer, you will not forget that I am an artist."

"I don't forget that you profess to be one, Mr. Marsh."

This was retort with a vengeance. Clifford reddened slightly, and looked angry. Mrs.

Denyer had reached the point to which her remarks were from the first directed, and it was not her intention to spare the young man's susceptibilities. She had long ago gauged him, and not inaccurately on the whole ; it seemed to her that he was of the men who can be " managed."

" I fail to understand you," said Marsh, with dignity.

" My dear Clifford, let me speak to you as one who has your well-being much at heart. I had no wish to hurt your feelings, but I have been upset by this silly affair, and it makes me speak a little sharply. Now, I see well enough what you have been about ; it is an old device of young gentlemen who wish to revenge themselves just a little for what they think a slight. Of course you have never given a thought to Miss Doran, who, as you say, would never dream of carrying on a flirtation, for she knows how things are between you and Madeline, and she is a young lady of very proper behaviour. In no case, as you of

course understand, could she be so indelicate
as anything of this kind would imply. No;
but you are vexed with Madeline about
some silly little difference, and you play
with her feelings. There has been enough
of it; I must interfere. And now let us
talk a little about your position. Madeline
has, of course, told me everything. Listen
to me, my dear Clifford; you must at once
accept Mr. Hibbert's kindly meant proposal
—you must indeed."

Marsh had reflected anxiously during this
speech. He let a moment of silence pass;
then said gravely:

"I cannot consent to do anything of the
kind, Mrs. Denyer."

"Oh yes, you can and will, Clifford.
Silly boy, don't you see that in this way you
secure yourself the future just suited to
your talents? As an artist, you will never
make your way; that is certain. As a man
with a substantial business at your back, you
can indulge your artistic tastes quite sufficiently, and will make yourself the centre of

an admiring circle. We cannot all be stars of the first magnitude. Be content to shine in a provincial sphere, at all events for a time. Madeline, as your wife, will help you substantially. You will have good society, and better the richer you become. You are made to be a rich man and to enjoy life. Now let us settle this affair with your step-father."

Still Clifford reflected, and again with the result that he appeared to have no thought of being persuaded to such concessions. The debate went on for a long time, ultimately with no little vigour on both sides. Its only immediate result was that Marsh left the house for a few days, retiring to meditate at Pompeii.

In the mean time, there was no apparent diminution in Madeline's friendliness towards Cecily Doran. It was not to be supposed that Madeline thought tenderly of the other's beauty, or with warm admiration of her endowments; but she would not let Clifford Marsh imagine that it mattered to her in the

least if he at once transferred his devotion
to Miss Doran. Her tone in conversing with
Cecily became a little more patronizing,—
though she spoke no more of impressionism,
—in proportion as she discovered the
younger girl's openness of mind and her
lack of self-assertiveness.

"You play the piano, I think?" she said
one day.

"For my own amusement only."

"And you draw?"

"With the same reserve."

"Ah," said Madeline, "I have long since
given up these things. Don't you think it
is a pity to make a pastime of an art? I
soon saw that I was never likely really to
do anything in music or drawing, and out
of respect for them I ceased to—to potter.
Please don't think I apply that word to you."

"Oh, but it is very applicable," replied
Cecily, with a laugh. "I think you are
quite right; I often enough have the same
feeling. But I am full of inconsistencies—
as you are finding out, I know."

Mrs. Lessingham displayed good nature in her intercourse with the Denyers. She smiled in private, and of course breathed to Cecily a word of warning ; but the family entertained her, and Madeline she came really to like. With Mrs. Denyer she compared notes on the Italy of other days.

"A sad, sad change !" Mrs. Denyer was wont to sigh. "All the poetry gone ! Think of Rome before 1870, and what it is now becoming. One never looked for intellect in Italy—living intellect, of course, I mean—but natural poetry one did expect and find. It is heart-breaking, this progress ! If it were not for my dear girls, I shouldn't be here ; they adore Italy—of course, never having known it as it was. And I am sure you must feel, as I do, Mrs. Lessingham, the miserable results of cheapened travel. Oh, the people one sees at railway-stations, even meets in hotels, I am sorry to say, sometimes ! In a few years, I do believe, Genoa and Venice will strongly remind one of Margate."

No echo of the cry of "Wolf!" ever sounded in Mrs. Denyer's conversation when she spoke of her husband. That Odysseus of commerce was always referred to as being concerned in enterprises of mysterious importance and magnitude; she would hint that he had political missions, naturally not to be spoken of in plain terms. Mrs. Lessingham often wondered with a smile what the truth really was; she saw no reason for making conjectures of a disagreeable kind, but it was pretty clear to her that selfishness, idleness, and vanity were at the root of Mrs. Denyer's character, and in a measure explained the position of the family.

During the last few days, Barbara had exhibited a revival of interest in the "place in Lincolnshire." Her experiments proved that it needed but a moderate ingenuity to make Mr. Musselwhite's favourite topic practically inexhaustible. The "place" itself having been sufficiently described, it was natural to inquire what other "places"

were its neighbours, what were the characteristics of the nearest town, how long it
took to drive from the "place" to the
town, from the "place" to such another
"place," and so on. Mr. Musselwhite was
undisguisedly grateful for every remark or
question that kept him talking at his ease.
It was always his dread lest a subject
should be broached on which he could say
nothing whatever — there were so many
such!—and as often as Barbara broke a
silence without realizing his fear, he glanced
at her with the gentlest and most amiable
smile. Never more than glanced; yet this
did not seem to be the result of shyness;
rather it indicated a lack of mental activity,
of speculation, of interest in her as a human
being.

One morning he lingered at the luncheon-
table when nearly all the others had withdrawn, playing with crumbs, and doubtless
shrinking from the *ennui* that lay before
him until dinner-time. Near him, Mrs.
Denyer, Barbara, and Zillah were standing

in conversation about some photographs that had this morning come by post.

"This one isn't at all like you, my dear," said Mrs. Denyer, with emphasis, to her eldest girl. "The other is passable, but I wouldn't have any of these."

"Well, of course I am no judge," replied Barbara, "but I can't agree with you. I much prefer this one."

Mr. Musselwhite was slowly rising.

"Let us take some one else's opinion," said the mother. "I wonder what Mr. Musselwhite would say?"

The mention of his name caused him to turn his head, half absently, with an inquiring smile. Barbara withdrew a step, but Mrs. Denyer, in the most natural way possible, requested Mr. Musselwhite's judgment on the portraits under discussion.

He took the two in his hands, and, after inspecting them, looked round to make comparison with the original. Barbara met his gaze placidly, with gracefully poised head, her hands joined behind her. It was such

a long time before the arbiter found anything to remark, that the situation became
a little embarrassing; Zillah laughed girl-
ishly, and her sister's eyes fell.

"Really, it's very hard to decide," said
Mr. Musselwhite at length, with grave conscientiousness. "I think they're both remarkably good. I really think I should
have some of both."

"Barbara thinks that this makes her
look too childish," said Mrs. Denyer, using
her daughter's name with a pleasant fa-
miliarity.

Again Mr. Musselwhite made close comparisons. It was, in fact, the first time
that he had seen the girl's features;
hitherto they had been, like everything else
not embalmed in his memory, a mere vague
perception, a detail of the phantasmic world
through which he struggled against his *ennui*.

"Childish? Oh dear, no!" he remarked,
almost vivaciously. "It is charming; they
are both charming. Really, I'd have some
of both, Miss Denyer."

"Then we certainly will," was Mrs. Denyer's conclusion; and with a gracious inclination of the head, she left the room, followed by her daughters. Mr. Musselwhite looked round for another glance at Barbara, but of course he was just too late.

Poor Madeline, in the mean time, was being sorely tried. Whilst Clifford Marsh was away at Pompeii, daily "scenes" took place between her and her mother. Mrs. Denyer would have had her make conciliatory movements, whereas Madeline, who had not exchanged a word with Clifford since the parting in wrath, was determined not to be the first to show signs of yielding. And she held her ground, tearless, resentful, strong in a sense of her own importance.

When he again took his place at Madame Glück's table, Clifford had the air of a man who has resigned himself to the lack of sympathy and appreciation—nay, who defies everything external, and in the strength of his genius goes serenely onwards. Never had he displayed such self-consciousness;

not for an instant did he forget to regulate
the play of his features. Mrs. Denyer he had
greeted distantly ; her daughters, more distantly still. He did not look more than
once or twice in Miss Doran's direction, for
Mrs. Denyer's reproof had made him conscious of an excess in artistic homage. His
neighbour being Mr. Bradshaw, he conversed with him agreeably, smiling seldom.
He seemed neither depressed nor uneasy ;
his countenance wore a grave and noble
melancholy, now and then illumined with
an indescribable ardour.

The Bradshaws had begun to talk of
leaving Naples, but this seemed to be the
apology for enjoying themselves which is
so characteristic of English people. § Even
Mrs. Bradshaw found her life from day to
day very pleasant, and in consequence never
saw her friends at the villa without expressing much uneasiness about affairs at home,
and blaming her husband for making so
long a stay. Both of them were now
honoured with the special attention of Mr.

Marsh. Clifford was never so much in his element as when conversing of art and kindred matters with persons who avowed their deficiencies in that sphere of knowledge, yet were willing to learn; relieved from the fear of criticism, he expanded, he glowed, he dogmatized. With Mrs. Lessingham he could not be entirely at his ease; her eye was occasionally disturbing to a pretender who did not lack discernment. But in walking about the museum with Mr. Bradshaw, he was the most brilliant of ciceroni. Jacob was not wholly credulous, for he had spoken of the young man with Mrs. Lessingham, but he found such companionship entertaining enough from time to time, and Clifford's knowledge of Italian was occasionally a help to him.

A day or two of moderate intimacy with any person whatsoever always led Clifford to a revelation of his private circumstances; it was not long before Mr. Bradshaw was informed not only of Mr. Hibbert's harshness, but of the painful treatment to which

Clifford was being subjected at the hands of Mrs. Denyer and Madeline. The latter point was handled with a good deal of tact, for Clifford had it in view that through Mr. Bradshaw his words would one way or other reach Mrs. Lessingham, and so perchance come to Miss Doran's ears. He made no unworthy charges; he spoke not in anger, but in sorrow; he was misunderstood, he was depreciated, by those who should have devoted themselves to supporting his courage under adversity. And as he talked, he became the embodiment of calm magnanimity; the rhetoric which was meant to impress his listener had an exalting effect upon himself—as usual.

"You mean to hold out, then?" asked the bluff Jacob, with a smile which all but became a chuckle.

"I am an artist," was the noble reply. "I cannot abandon my life's work."

"But how about bread and cheese? They are necessary to an artist, as much as to other men, I'm afraid."

Clifford smiled calmly.

" I shall not be the first who has starved in such a cause."

Jacob roared as he related this conversation to his wife.

" I must keep an eye on the lad," he said. " When I hear he's given in, I'll write him a letter of congratulation."

CHAPTER VIII.

PROOF AGAINST ILLUSION.

An interesting conversation took place one morning between Mrs. Spence and Mrs. Lessingham with regard to Cecily. They were alone together at the villa ; Cecily and Miriam had gone for a drive with the Bradshaws. After speaking of Reuben Elgar, Mrs. Lessingham passed rather abruptly to what seemed a disconnected subject.

"I don't think it's time yet for Cecily to give up her set studies. I should like to find some one to read with her regularly again before long—say Latin and history ; there would be no harm in a little mathematics. But there's a difficulty in finding the suitable person." She smiled. "I'm afraid only a lady will answer the purpose."

"Better, no doubt," assented Eleanor, also with a smile.

"And ladies who would be any good to Cecily are not at one's disposition every day. What an admirable mind she has! I never knew any one acquire with so little effort. Of course, she has long ago left me behind in everything. The only use I can be to her is to help her in gaining knowledge of the world—not to be learnt entirely out of books, we know."

"What is your system with her?"

"You see that I have one," said Mrs. Lessingham, gratified, and rustling her plumage a little as a lady does when she is about to speak in confidence of something that pleases her. "Of course, I very soon understood that the ordinary *surveillance* and restrictions and moral theories were of little use in her case. (I may speak with you quite freely, I am sure.) I'm afraid the results would have been very sad if Cecily had grown up in Lancashire."

"I doubt whether she would have grown up at all."

"Indeed, it seemed doubtful. If her strength had not utterly failed, she must have suffered dreadfully in mind. I studied her carefully during the first two years; then I was able to pursue my method with a good deal of confidence. It has been my aim to give free play to all her faculties; to direct her intelligence, but never to check its growth—as is commonly done. We know what is meant by a girl's education, as a rule; it is not so much the imparting of knowledge as the careful fostering of special ignorances. I think I put it rightly?"

"I think so."

"It is usual to say that a girl must know nothing of this and that and the other thing—these things being, in fact, the most important for her to understand. I won't say that every girl can safely be left so free as I have left Cecily; but when one has to deal with exceptional intelligence, why not yield it the exceptional advantages? Then again, I had to bear in mind that Cecily has strong emotions. This seemed to me only another reason for releasing her mind from the misconceptions it is usual to encourage. I have done my best to help her to see things as they *are*, not as moral teachers would like them to be, and as parents make-believe to their girls that they are indeed."

Mrs. Lessingham ended on a suave note of triumph, and smiled very graciously as Eleanor looked approval.

"The average parent says," she pursued, "that his or her daughter must be kept pure-minded, and therefore must grow up in a fool's paradise. I have no less liking for purity, but I understand it in rather a different sense; certain examples of the common purity that I have met with didn't entirely recommend themselves to me. Then again, the average parent says that the daughter's lot in life is marriage, and that after marriage is time enough for her to throw away the patent rose-coloured spectacles. I, on the other hand, should be very sorry indeed to think that Cecily has no lot in life besides marriage ; to me she seemed a human being to be instructed and developed, not a pretty girl to be made ready for the market. The rose-coloured spectacles had no part whatever in my system. I have known some who threw them aside at marriage, in the ordinary way, with the result that they thenceforth looked on everything very obliquely indeed. I'm sorry to say that it was my own fate to wear those spectacles, and I know only too well how hard a struggle it cost me to recover healthy eyesight."

" Mine fell off and got broken long before I was married," said Eleanor, "and my parents didn't think it worth while buying new ones."

" Wise parents ! No, I have steadily re-sisted the theory that a girl must know nothing, think nothing, but what is likely to meet the approval of the average husband —that is to say, the foolish, and worse than foolish, husband. I see no such difference between girl and boy as demands a difference in moral training; we know what comes of the prevalent contrary views. And in Cecily's case, I believe I have vindicated my theory. She respects herself; she knows all that lack of self-respect involves. She has been fed on wholesome victuals, not on adulterated milk. She is not haunted with that vulgar shame which passes for maiden modesty. Do you find fault with her, as a girl?"

"I should have to ponder long for an objection."

"And what is the practical result? In whatever society she is, I am quite easy in mind about her. Cecily will never do anything foolish. It's only the rose-coloured spectacles that cause stumbling. And I mean by 'stumbling' all the silliness to which girls are subject. Ah! if I could live *my* girlhood over again, and with some sensible woman to guide me! If I could have been put on my guard against idiotic illusions, as Cecily is!"

"We mustn't expect too much of education," Eleanor ventured to remark. "There is no way of putting experience into a young girl's head. It would say little for her qualities if a girl could not make a generous mistake."

"Such mistakes are not worthy of being called generous, as a rule. They are too imbecile. That state of illusion is too contemptible. There is very little danger of Cecily's seeing any one in a grossly false light."

Eleanor did not at once assent.

"You seem to doubt that?" added the other, with a searching look.

"I think she is as well guarded as a girl can be; but, as I said before, education is no substitute for experience. Don't think me captious, however. I sympathize entirely with the course you have taken. If I had a daughter, I should like her to be brought up on the same principles."

"Cecily is very mature for her age," continued Mrs. Lessingham, with evident pleasure in stating and restating her grounds of confidence. "She feels strongly, but never apart from judgment. Now and then she astonishes me with her discernment of character; clearness of thought seems almost to anticipate in her the experience on which you lay such stress. Have you noticed her with Mr. Mallard? How differently many girls would behave! But Cecily understands him so well; she knows he thinks of her as a child, and nothing could be more simply natural than her friendship for him. I suppose Mr. Mallard is one of the artists who never marry?"

"I don't know him well enough to decide that," answered Eleanor, with a curious smile.

It was in the evening of this day, when the Spences and Miriam were sitting together after dinner, that a servant announced a visit of Reuben Elgar, adding that he was in his sister's room. Miriam went to join him.

"You can spare me a minute or two?" he asked cheerily, as she entered.

"Certainly. You are just back from Pompeii?"

"From Castellammare—from Sorrento the indescribable—from Amalfi the unimaginable—from Salerno! Leave Naples without seeing those places, and hold yourself for ever the most wretched of mortals! Old Mallard forced me to go with him, and I am in his debt to eternity!"

This exalted manner of speech was little to Miriam's taste, especially from her brother. Sobriety was what she desired in him. It seemed a small advantage that his extravagance should exhibit itself in this way rather than in worse; the danger was still there.

"Sit down, and talk more quietly. You say Mr. Mallard *forced* you to go?"

"I was coming back to Naples from Pompeii. By-the-bye, I went up Vesuvius, and descended shoeless. The guides ought to have metal boots on hire. I was coming back, but Mallard clutched me by the coat-collar. Even now I've come sorely against

his will. I left him at Amalfi. I'm going
to settle my affairs here to-morrow, and join
him again. He's persuaded me to try and
work at Amalfi."

"How long do you think of staying
there ?"

"It all depends. Perhaps I shan't be
able to do anything, after all."

"But surely that depends on yourself."

"Not a bit! If I were a carpenter or
bricklayer, one might say so—in a sense.
But such work as I am going to do is a
question of mood, influences, caprices——"

Miriam reflected.

"Mr. Mallard was unwilling to let you
return here ?"

"Naturally. He knows my uncertainty.
But I have promised him ; I shall keep my
word."

"He is working himself ?"

"Will be by now ; we had a horrible
day of rain at Amalfi. He seems rather
glummer than usual, but that won't hinder
his work. I wish I had the old fellow's

energy. After all, though, one can force one's self to use pencils and brushes; it's a different thing when all has to come from the brain. If you haven't a quiet mind——"

"What disturbs you?" Miriam asked, watching him.

"Oh, there's always something. I wish you could give me a share of your equanimity. Never mind, I shall try. By-the-by, I ought to have a word with Mrs. Lessingham and Cecily before I go. Are they likely to be here to-morrow?"

"I can't say."

"Then I shall call at their place. When will they be at home?"

"Do you think you ought to do that?" Miriam asked, without looking at him.

"Why on earth not?"

His brow darkened, and he seemed about to utter something not unlike his vehemencies on the day of arrival.

"You must judge for yourself, of course," said Miriam. "We won't talk about it."

Reuben nodded agreement carelessly. Then he began to talk of his proposed work, and presently they went to join the Spences. For an hour or more, Reuben held forth rapturously on what he had seen these last few days. He could not rest seated, but paced up and down the room, gesticulating, fervidly eloquent.

"Do play me something, will you, Mrs. Spence?" he asked at length. (His cousinship with Eleanor had never been affirmed by intimate association, and he had not the habit of addressing her by the personal name). "Just for ten minutes; then I'll be off and trouble you no more. Something to invigorate! A rugged piece!"

Eleanor made a choice from Beethoven, and, whilst she played, Elgar leant forward on the back of a chair. Then he bade them good-bye, his pulse at fever-time.

Half-past ten next morning found him walking hither and thither on the Mergellina, frequently consulting his watch. He decided at length to approach the house in which his acquaintances dwelt. Passing through the *portone*, whom should he encounter but Clifford Marsh, known to him only from the casual meeting at Pompeii, not by name. They stopped to speak. Elgar inquired if the other lived at Madame Glück's.

" For the present."

" I have friends here," Reuben added. " You know Mrs. Lessingham ? "

" Oh yes," replied Clifford, eyeing his collocutor. " If you are calling to see those ladies," he continued, " they went out half an hour ago. I saw them drive away."

Elgar muttered his annoyance. Though he disliked doing so, he asked Marsh whether he knew when the ladies were likely to return. Clifford declared his ignorance. The two looked at each other, smiled, said good morning, and turned different ways.

Reuben walked about the sea-front for a couple of hours. " Who is that confounded fellow ? " he kept asking in his mind, adding the highly ludicrous question, "What business has he to know them?" His impatience waxed; now and then he strode at such a pace that perspiration covered him. The most trivial discomposure had often much the same effect on him; if he happened to have a difficulty in finding his way, for instance, he would fume himself into exasperated heat.

"What business have they to live in a vulgar boarding-house? It's abominable bad taste and indiscretion in that woman. In fact, I don't like Mrs. Lessingham.—And what the devil has it to do with me?"

He strode up to the villa. Possibly they were there; yet he didn't like to call—for various reasons. He fretted about the roads, this way and that, till hunger oppressed him. Having eaten at the first restaurant he came to, he directed his steps towards the Mergellina again. At two o'clock he reached the house and made inquiry. The ladies had not yet returned.

He struck off towards the Chiaia, again

paced backwards and forwards, cursed at
carriage-drivers who plagued him, tried to
amuse himself on the Santa Lucia. And
pray what was all this fuss about? When
he rose this morning, he had half a mind to
start at once for Amalfi, and not see Mrs.
Lessingham and her niece at all; he "didn't
know that he cared much." He had met
Cecily Doran twice. The second time was
on the Strada Nuova di Posilipo, where he
encountered a carriage in which Cecily and
her aunt were taking the air; he talked
with them for three minutes. It was the
undeniable fact that he had broken away
from "old Mallard" merely to see Cecily
again. He had never tried to blind himself
to it; that kind of thing was not in his
way. None the less was it a truth that he
thought himself capable of saying good-bye
to the wonderful girl, and posting off to his
literary work. Why expose himself to
temptation? Because he chose to; because
it was pleasant; surely an excellent reason.

If only he hadn't come up against that

confounded artist-fellow! That had upset him, most absurdly. A half good-looking sort of fellow; a fellow who could prate with a certain *brio;* not unlikely to make something of a figure in the eyes of a girl like Cecily. And what then?

Before now, Elgar had confessed to a friend that he couldn't read the marriage-column in a newspaper without feeling a distinct jealousy of all the male creatures there mentioned.

He sought out a *caffè,* and sat there for an hour, drinking a liquor that called itself lacryma-Christi, but would at once have been detected for a pretender by a trained palate. He drank it for the first time, and tried to enjoy it, but his mind kept straying to alien things. When it was nearly four o'clock, he again went forth, took a carriage, and bade the man drive quickly.

This time he was successful. A servant conducted him by many stairs and passages to Mrs. Lessingham's sitting-room. He entered, and found himself alone with Cecily.

"Mrs. Lessingham will certainly be back very soon," she said, in shaking hands with him. "They told me you had called before, and I thought you would like better to wait a few minutes than to be disappointed again."

"I think of going to Amalfi to-morrow morning, perhaps for a long time," remarked the visitor. "I wished to say good-bye."

The accumulated impatience and nervousness of the whole morning disturbed his pulses and put a weight upon his tongue; he spoke with awkward indecision, held himself awkwardly. His own voice sounded boorish to him after Cecily's accents.

Cecily began to speak of how she had spent the day. Her aunt was making purchases—was later in returning than had been expected. Then she asked for an account of Elgar's doings since they last met. The conversation grew easier; Reuben began to recover his natural voice, and to lose disagreeable self-consciousness in the delight of hearing Cecily and meeting her look. Had he known her better, he would have observed that she spoke with unusual diffidence, that she was not quite so self-possessed as of wont, and that her manner was deficient in the frank gaiety which as a rule made its great charm. Her tone softened itself in questioning; she listened so attentively that, when he had ceased speaking, her eyes always rose to his, as if she had expected something further.

"Who is the young artist that lives here?" Elgar inquired. "I met him at Pompeii, and to-day came upon him here in the courtyard. A slight, rather boyish fellow."

"I think you mean Mr. Marsh," replied Cecily, smiling. "He has recently been at Pompeii, I know."

"You are on friendly terms with him?"

"Not on *unfriendly*," she answered, with amusement.

Elgar averted his face. Instantly the flow of his blood was again turbid; he felt an inclination to fling out some ill-mannered remark.

"You must come in contact with all kinds of odd people in a place like this."

"One or two are certainly odd," was the reply, in a gentle tone; "but most of them are very pleasant to be with occasionally. Naturally we see more of the Bradshaws than of any one else. There's a family named Denyer—a lady with three daughters; I don't think you would dislike them. Mr. Marsh is their intimate friend."

It was all but as though she pleaded against a mistaken judgment which troubled her. To Mallard she had spoken of her fellow-boarders in quite a different way, with merry though kindly criticism, or in the strain of generous idealization which so often marked her language.

"Do you know anything of his work?" Elgar pursued.

"I have seen a few of his water-colour drawings."

"He showed you them?"

"No; one of the Miss Denyers did. He had given them to her."

"Oh!" He at once brightened. "And how did they strike you?"

"I'm sorry to say they didn't interest me much. But I have no right to sit in judgment."

Elgar had the good taste to say nothing more on the subject. He let his eyes rest on her down-turned face for a moment.

"You see a good deal of Miriam, I'm glad to hear."

"I am sometimes afraid I trouble her by going too often."

"Have no such fear. I wish you were living under the same roof with her. No one's society could do her so much good as yours. The poor girl has too long been in need of such an aid to rational cheerfulness."

They were interrupted by the entrance of an English maid-servant, who asked whether Miss Doran would have tea brought at once, or wait till Mrs. Lessingham's return.

"You see how English we are," said Cecily to her visitor. "I think we'll have it now; Mrs. Lessingham may be here any moment."

It was growing dusk. Whilst the conversation was diverted by trifles, two lighted lamps were brought into the room. Elgar had risen and gone to the window.

"We won't shut out the evening sky," said Cecily, standing not far from him.

The door closed upon the servant who had carried in the tea-tray. Elgar turned to his companion, and said in a musing tone, with a smile :

"How long is it since we saw each other every day in Manchester ?"

"Seven years since that short time you spent with us."

"Seven ; yes. You were not twelve then ; I was not quite twenty-one. As regards change, a lifetime might have passed since, with both of us. Yet I don't feel very old, not oppressively ancient."

"And I'm sure I don't."

They laughed together.

"You are younger than you were then," he continued, in his most characteristic voice, the voice which was musical and alluring, and suggestive of his nature's passionate depths and heights. "You have grown into health of body and soul, and out of all the evil things that would have robbed you of natural happiness. Nothing ever made me more glad than first seeing you at the villa. I didn't know what you had become, and in looking at you I rejoiced on your account. You would gladden even miserable old age, like sunlight on a morning of spring."

Cecily moved towards the tea-table in silence. She began to fill one of the cups, but put the teapot down again and waited for a moment. Having resumed her purpose, she looked round and saw Elgar seated sideways on a chair by the window. With the cup of tea in her hand, she approached him and offered it without speaking. He rose quickly to take it, and went to another part of the room.

"I hope Miriam will stay here the whole winter," Cecily said, as she seated herself by the table.

" I hope so," he assented absently, putting his tea aside. " How long are you and Mrs. Lessingham likely to stay ? "

" At least till February, I think."

" Shall you get as far as Amalfi some day ? "

" Oh yes! And Miriam will come with us, I hope. And to Capri too."

" I must see Capri. I shouldn't wonder if I go there soon ; probably it would suit my purpose better than Amalfi. Yet I must be alone, if I am to work. I haven't Mallard's detachment. That seems to you a paltry confession of weakness."

" No, indeed. I am told that Mr. Mallard is quite exceptional in his power of disregarding everything but his work."

" Exceptional in many things, no doubt. I must seem very insignificant in comparison."

" Why should you ? Mr. Mallard is so much older ; he has long been fixed in his course."

" Older, yes," assented Elgar, with satisfaction. "Perhaps at his age I too may have done something worth doing."

"Who could doubt it?"

"It does me good to hear you say that!" He moved from his distant place, and threw himself in one of his usual careless attitudes on a nearer chair. "But Miriam has no faith in me, not a jot! Does she speak harshly of me to you?"

"No."

Cecily shook her head, and seemed unable to speak more than the monosyllable.

"But she has nothing encouraging to say? She shows that she looks upon me as one of whom no good can come? That is the impression you have received from her?"

Cecily looked at him gravely.

"She has scarcely spoken of you at all—scarcely more than the few words that were inevitable."

"In itself a condemnation."

Cecily was mute. Before Elgar could say anything more, the door opened. With a sudden radiance on her features, the girl

looked up to greet Mrs. Lessingham's entrance.

" How long you have been, aunt ! "

" Yes ; I am sorry. How do you do, Mr.
Elgar ? Tea, Cecily, lest I perish ! "

From the doorway her quick glance had
scrutinized both the young people. Of course
she betrayed no surprise ; neither did she
make exhibition of pleasure. Her greeting
of the visitor was gracefully casual, given
in passing. She sank upon a low chair as
if overcome with weariness. Mrs. Lessingham had nothing to learn in the arts where-
with social intercourse is kept smooth in spite
of nature's improprieties. When she chose,
she could be the awe-inspiring chaperon, no
less completely than she was at other times
the contemner of the commonplace.

" So you leave us to-morrow, Mr. Elgar ?
I have just met Mr. Spence, and heard the
news from him. I am glad you could find
a moment to call. You are going to be
very busy, I hear, for the rest of the
winter."

"I hope so," Elgar replied, walking across the room to fetch his half-emptied teacup.

"We shall look eagerly for the results of your work."

For ten minutes the conversation kept a rather flat course. Cecily only spoke when addressed by her aunt; then quite in her usual way. Elgar took the first opportunity to signal departure. When Cecily gave him her hand, it was with a moment's unfaltering look—a look very different from that which charmed everyday acquaintances at their coming and going, unlike anything man or woman had yet seen on her countenance. The faintest smile hovered about her lips as she said, "Good-bye;" her steadfast eyes added the hope which there was no need to speak.

When he was gone, Mrs. Lessingham sipped her tea in silence. Cecily moved about, and presently brought a book to her chair by the tea-table.

"No doubt you had the advantage of hearing Mr. Elgar's projects detailed," said her aunt, with irony which presumed a complete understanding between them.

"No." Cecily shook her head and smiled.

"Curious how closely he and Mr. Marsh resemble each other at times."

"Do you think so?"

"Haven't you noticed it? There are differences, of course. Mr. Elgar is originally much better endowed; though at present I should think he is even less to be depended upon, either intellectually or morally. But they belong to the same species. What numbers of such young men I have met!"

"What are the characteristics of the species, aunt?" Cecily inquired, with a pleasant laugh.

"I dare say you know them almost as well as I do. You might write an essay on 'The Young Man of Promise' of our day. I should be rather too severe; you would treat them with a lighter hand, and therefore more effectually."

In speaking, she kept her eyes on the

girl, who appeared to muse the subject with sportful malice.

"I am not sure," said Cecily, "that Mr. Elgar would come into the essay."

"You mean that his promise is too obviously delusive?"

"Not exactly that. I rather think he should have an essay to himself."

"Of what tendency?" asked Mrs. Lessingham, still closely observant.

"Oh, it would need much meditation; but I think I could make it interesting."

With another laugh, she dismissed the subject; nor did her aunt endeavour to revive it.

The morrow was Sunday. Elgar knew at what time his train left for Salerno; the time-table was the same as for other days. Yet he lay in bed till nearly noon, till the train had long since started. No, he should not go to-day.

It irked him to rise at all. He had not slept; his head was hot, and his hands shook

nervously. Dressed, he sat down for a
minute, and remained seated half an hour,
gazing at the wall. When at length he
left the house, he walked without seeing
anything, stumbling against things and
people.

Of course, he knew last night that there
was no journey for him to-day. Promise?
A promise is void when its fulfilment has
become impossible. Very likely Mallard
had a conviction that he would not come
back at the appointed time. To-morrow,
perhaps; and perhaps not even to-morrow.
It had got beyond his control.

He ate, and returned to his room. Just
now his need was physical repose, undis-
turbed indulgence of reverie. And the
reverie of a man in his condition is a
singular process. It consists of a small
number of memories, forecasts, imaginings,
repeated over and over again, till one would
think the brain must weary itself beyond
endurance. It can go on for many hours
consecutively, and not only remain a suffi-

cient and pleasurable employment, but render every other business repulsive, all but impossible.

At evening there came a change. He was now unable to keep still; he went into the town, and exhausted himself with walking up and down the hilly streets. Society would have helped him, but he could find none. He would not go to the villa; still less could he visit the boarding-house.

What a night! At times he moved about his room like one in frantic pain, finally flinging himself upon the bed and lying there till the impulse of his fevered mind broke the beginnings of sleep. Or he walked the length of the floor, with measured step, fifty times, counting each time he turned— a sort of conscious insanity. Or he took his pocket-knife, and drove the point into the flesh of his arm, satisfied when the pang became intolerable. Then again a loss of all control in mere frenzy, the desire to shout, to yell. . . .

Oh, good, happy, respectable people!

How kindly did Nature deal with you, when
she framed you to be placid and useful members of society—to fall becomingly in love
at five and twenty, and wait peacefully for
marriage in the ninth year after, when your
means are adequate ; to see children grow
up about you as your hairs grizzle, and
witness in them the repetition of your own
orderly youth !   Right is it, right and good,
that you should kneel at your bedsides and
render thanks for the day of prose that has
been granted you.   In prose is your blessed-
ness ; seek to know nothing else ; shun the
poet and all his works as you do the devil
with whom you are theoretically so familiar.
You might have been born with a core of
fire in your bosoms, instead of that ingenious organ which pumps the gentle current
of life along your unfretted veins.   Think
of it, and render double thanks. . . .

Elgar was out of the house at sunrise.
He went down to the Chiaia, loitered this
way and that, always in the end turning
towards Posilipo.   He drank his coffee, but

ate nothing; then again walked along the sea-front. Between nine and ten he turned into the upward road, and went with purpose towards Villa Sannazaro.

CHAPTER IX.

IN THE DEAD CITY.

THOUGH it was Sunday, Cecily resolved to go and spend the afternoon with Miriam. She was restless, and could not take pleasure in Mrs. Lessingham's conversation. Possibly her arrival at the villa would be anything but welcome; but she must see Miriam.

She drove up by herself, and first of all saw the Spences. From them she learnt that Miriam, as usual on Sunday, was keeping her own room.

"Do you think I may venture, Mrs. Spence?"

"Go and announce yourself, my dear. If you are bidden avaunt, come back and cheer us old people with your brightness."

So Cecily went with light step along the corridor, and with light fingers tapped at

Miriam's room. The familiar voice bade her enter. Miriam was sitting near the window, on her lap a closed book.

"May I —— ?"

"Of course you may," was the quiet answer.

Cecily closed the door, came forward, and bent to kiss her friend. Then she glanced at the "St. Cecilia;" then examined herself for a moment in one of the mirrors; then took off her hat, mantle, and gloves.

"I want to stay as long as your patience will suffer me."

"Do so."

"You avoid saying how long that is likely to be."

"How can I tell?"

"Oh, you have experience of me. You know how trying you find me in certain moods. To-day I am in a very strange mood indeed; very malicious, very wicked. And it is Sunday."

Miriam did not seem to resent this. She looked away at the window, but smiled.

Could Cecily have been aware how her face had changed when the door opened, she would not have doubted whether she was truly welcome.

"What book is that, Miriam?"

Cecily had been half afraid to ask; to her surprise it proved to be Dante.

"Do you read this on Sunday?"

Miriam deigned no reply. The other, sitting just in front of her, took up the volume and rustled its leaves.

"How far have you got? This pencil-mark? 'Amor ch'a null' amato amar perdona.'"

She read the line in an undertone, slowly towards the close. Miriam's face showed a sudden and curious emotion. Glancing at the book, she said abruptly:

"No; that's an old mark—a difficulty I had. I'm long past that."

"So am I. 'Amor ch'a null'——'"

Miriam stretched out her hand and took the volume with impatience.

"I'm at the end of this canto," she said,

pointing. "Never mind it now. I should have thought you would have gone somewhere, such a fine afternoon."

"That sounds remarkably like a hint that patience is near its end."

"I didn't mean it for that."

"Then let us get a carriage and drive somewhere together, we two alone."

Miriam shook her head.

"Because it is Sunday?" asked Cecily, with a mischievous smile, leaning her head aside.

"There is an understanding between us, Cecily. Don't break it."

"But I told you my mood was wicked. I feel disposed to break any and every undertaking. I should like to fret and torment and offend you. I should like to ask you why *I* am allowed to enjoy the sunshine, and you not? *Oggi è festa!* What a dreadful sound that must have in your ears, Miriam!"

"But they don't apply it to Sunday," returned the other, who seemed to resign herself to this teasing.

" Indeed they do ! " With a sudden change of subject, Cecily added, " Your brother came to see us yesterday, to say good-bye."

" Did he ?'

" It doesn't interest you. You care nothing where he goes, or what he does— nothing whatever, Miriam. He told me so ; but I knew it already."

" He told you so ? " Miriam asked, with cold surprise.

" Yes. You are unkind ; you are un- natural."

" And you, Cecily, are childish. I never knew you so childish as to-day."

" I warned you. He and I had a long talk before aunt came home."

" I'm sorry he should have thought it necessary to talk about himself."

" What more natural, when he is be- ginning a new portion of life ? Never mind ; we won't speak of it. May I play you a new piece I have learnt ? "

" Do you mean, of sacred music ? "

" Sacred ? Why, all music is sacred. There are tunes and jinglings that I shouldn't call so; but neither do I call them music, just as I distinguish between bad or foolish verse and poetry. Everything worthy of being called art is sacred. I shall keep telling you that till in self-defence you are forced to think about it And now I shall play the piece, whether you like or not."

She opened the piano. What she had in mind was one of the " Moments Musicaux" of Schubert—a strain of exquisite melody, which ceased too soon. Cecily sat for a few moments at the key-board after she had finished, her head bent; then she came and stood before Miriam.

"Do you like it ? "

There was no answer. She looked steadily at the troubled face, and, as it still kept averted from her, she sank upon her knees, and put her arms softly, half playfully, about Miriam's neck, and laid her head against her bosom.

"Why must there always be such a distance between us, Miriam dear? Even when I seem so near to you as this, what a deep black gulf really separates us!"

"You were once on my side of it," said Miriam, her voice softened. "How did you pass to the other?"

"How could I tell you? No one read me lectures, or taught me hard arguments. The change came insensibly, like passing out of a dream into the light of morning. I followed where my nature led, and my thoughts about everything altered. I don't know how it might have been if I had lived on with you. But my happiness was not there."

"Happiness!" murmured the other, scornfully.

"A word you don't, won't understand. Yet to me it means much. Who knows? Perhaps there may come a day when I look back upon it, and see it as empty of satisfaction as it now seems to you. But more likely that I shall live to look back in sorrow for its loss."

The dialogue became such as they had held more than once of late, fruitless it seemed, only saddening to both. And Cecily was to-day saddened by it beyond her wont; her excessive gaiety yielded to a dejection which passed indeed, but for a while made her very unlike herself, silent, with troubled eyes.

"I had one valid excuse for coming to see you to-day," she said, when gaiety and dejection had both gone by. "Mr. and Mrs. Bradshaw seriously think of going to Rome at the end of next week, and they wish to have another day at Pompeii. They would like it so much if you would go with them. If you do, I also will; we shall make four for a carriage, and drive there, and come back by train."

"What day?"

"To-morrow, if it be fine. Let me take them your assent."

Miriam agreed.

On Monday morning, as arranged, she

was driving down to the Mergellina, when, with astonishment, she saw her brother standing by the roadside, beckoning to her. The carriage stopped, and he came up to speak.

"Where are you off to?" he asked.

"You are still here?"

"I haven't been well. Didn't feel able to go yesterday. I was just coming to see you."

"Not well, Reuben? Why didn't you come before?"

"I couldn't. I want to speak to you. Where are you going?"

She told him the plan for the day. Elgar turned aside, and meditated.

"I'll see you there—at Pompeii somewhere. It'll be on my way."

"I had rather not go at all. I'll ask them to excuse me; Mrs. Lessingham will perhaps take my place, and—— "

"No! I'll see you at Pompeii. I shall have no difficulty in finding you."

Miriam looked at him anxiously.

"I don't wish you to meet us there, Reuben."

"And I *do* wish! Let me have my way, Miriam. Say nothing about me, and let the meeting seem by chance."

"I can't do that. You make yourself ridiculous, after——"

"Let me judge for myself. Go on, or you'll be late."

She half rose, as if about to descend from the carriage. Elgar laid his hand on her arm, and clutched it so strongly that she sank back and regarded him with a look of anger.

"Miriam! Do as I wish, dear. Be kind to me for this once. If you refuse, it will make no difference. Have some feeling for me. This one day, Miriam."

Again she looked at him, and reflected. On account of the driver, though of course he could not understand them, they had subdued their voices, and Reuben's sudden action had not been noticeable.

"This one piece of sisterly kindness," he pleaded.

"It shall be as you wish," Miriam replied, her face cast down.

"Thank you, a thousand times. Avanti, cocchiere!"

Scrutiny less keen than Miriam's could perceive that Cecily had not her usual pleasure in to-day's expedition. Even Mrs. Bradshaw, sitting over against her in the carriage, noticed that the girl's countenance lacked its natural animation, wore now and then a tired look; the lids hung a little heavily over the beautiful eyes, and the checks were a thought pale. When she forgot herself in conversation, Cecily was the same as ever; mirthful, brightly laughing, fervent in expressing delight; but her thoughts too often made her silent, and then one saw that she was not heart and soul in the present. It was another Cecily than on that day at Baiæ. "She has been over-exciting herself since she came here," was Mrs. Bradshaw's mental remark. Miriam, anxiously observant, made a different interpretation, and was harassed with a painful conflict of thoughts.

Jacob Bush Bradshaw had no eyes for these trivialities. He sat in the squared posture of a hearty Englishman, amusing himself with everything they passed on the road, self-congratulant on the knowledge and experience he had been storing, joking as often as he spoke.

"The lad Marsh would have uncommonly liked an invitation to come with us to-day," he said, about mid-way in the drive. "What precious mischief we could have made by asking him, Hannah!"

"There's no room for him, fortunately."

"Oh yes; up on the box."

His eye twinkled as he looked at Cecily. She questioned him.

"Where would be the mischief, Mr. Bradshaw?"

"He talks nonsense, my dear," interposed Mrs. Bradshaw. "Pay no attention to him."

Miriam had heard now and then of

Clifford Marsh. She met Jacob's smile, and involuntarily checked it by her gravity.

"We might have asked the Denyers as well," said Cecily, "and have had another carriage, or gone by train."

Mr. Bradshaw chuckled for some minutes at this proposal, but his wife would not allow him to pursue the jest.

They had a luncheon at the Hôtel Diomède before entering the precincts of the ruins. Mr. Bradshaw had invariably a splendid appetite, and was by this time skilled in ordering the meals that suited him. The few phrases of Italian which he had appropriated were given forth *ore rotundo,* with Anglo-Saxon emphasis on the *o*'s, and accompanied with large gestures. His mere appearance always sufficed to put landlords and waiters into their most urbane mood; they never failed to take him for one of the English nobility—a belief confirmed by the handsomeness of his gratuities. Mrs. Bradshaw was not, perhaps, the ideal lady of rank, but the fine self-

satisfaction on her matronly visage, the
good-natured disdain with which she
allowed herself to be waited upon by foolish
foreigners, her solid disregard of everything
beyond the circle of her own party, were
impressive enough, and exacted no little
subservience.

Strong in the experience of two former
visits, Mr. Bradshaw would have no guide
to-day. Murray in hand, he knew just
what he wished to see again, and where to
find it. As Miriam was at Pompeii for the
first time, he took her especially under his
direction, and showed her the city much
as he might have led her over his silk-mill
in Manchester. Unimbued with history and
literature, he knew nothing of the scholar's
or the poet's enthusiasm; his gratification
lay in exercising his solid intelligence on a
lot of strange and often grotesque facts.
Here men had lived two thousand years
ago. There was no mistake about it; you
saw the deep ruts of their wheels along the
rugged streets; nay, you saw the wearing

of their very feet on the comically narrow
pavements. And their life had been as
different as possible from that of men in
Manchester. Everything excited him to
merriment.

"Now, this is the house of old Pansa—
no doubt an ancestor of friend Sancho"—
with a twinkle in his eye. "We'll go
over this carefully, Mrs. Baske; it's one
of the largest and completest in Pompeii.
Here we are in what they called the
atrium."

Cecily spoke seldom. Of course, she
would have preferred to be alone here
with Miriam; best of all—or nearly so—
if they could have made the same party as
at Baiæ. At times she lingered a little
behind the others, and seemed deep in con-
templation of some object; or she stood to
watch the lizards darting about the sunny
old walls. When all were enjoying the
view from the top of Jupiter's Temple, she
gazed long towards the Sorrento promontory, the height of St. Angelo.

"Amalfi is over on the far side," she said to Miriam. "They are both working there now."

Miriam replied nothing.

When they were in the Street of Tombs, Cecily again paused, by the sepulchre of the priestess Mamia, whence there is a clear prospect across the bay towards the mountains. Turning back again, she heard a voice that made her tremble with delighted surprise. A wall concealed the speaker from her; she took a few quick steps, and saw Reuben Elgar shaking hands with the Bradshaws. He looked at her, and came forward. She could not say anything, and was painfully conscious of the blood that rushed to her face; never yet had she known this stress of heart-beats that made suffering of joy, and the misery of being unable to command herself under observant eyes.

It was years since Elgar and the Bradshaws had met. As a boy he had often visited their house, but from the time of his leaving home at sixteen to go to a boarding-

school, his acquaintance with them, as with
all his other Manchester friends, practically
ceased. They had often heard of him—too
often, in their opinion. Aware of his arrival
at Naples, they had expressed no wish to
see him. Still, now that he met them in
this unexpected way, they could not but
assume friendliness. Jacob, not on the
whole intolerant, was willing enough to take
" the lad " on his present merits; Reuben
had the guise and manners of a gentleman,
and perhaps was grown out of his reprobate
habits. Mr. Bradshaw and his wife could
not but notice Cecily's agitation at the
meeting; they exchanged wondering glances,
and presently found an opportunity for a
few words apart. What was going on?
How had these two young folks become so
intimate? Well, it was no business of
theirs. Lucky that Mrs. Baske was one of
the company.

And why should Cecily disguise that now
only was her enjoyment of the day begun—
that only now had the sunshine its familiar

brightness, the ancient walls and ways their true enchantment? She did not at once become more talkative, but the shadow had passed utterly from her face, and there was no more listlessness in her movements.

"I have stopped here on my way to join Mallard," was all Reuben said, in explanation of his presence.

All kept together. Mr. Bradshaw resumed his interest in antiquities, but did not speak so freely about them as before.

"Your brother knows a good deal more about these things than I do, Mrs. Baske," he remarked. "He shall give us the benefit of his Latin."

Miriam resolutely kept her eyes alike from Reuben and from Cecily. Hitherto her attention to the ruins had been intermittent, but occasionally she had forgotten herself so far as to look and ponder; now she saw nothing. Her mind was gravely troubled; she wished only that the day were over.

As for Elgar, he seemed to the Bradshaws singularly quiet, modest, inoffensive. If he ventured a suggestion or a remark, it was in a subdued voice and with the most pleasant manner possible. He walked for a time with Mrs. Bradshaw, and accommodated himself with much tact to her way of regarding foreign things, whether ancient or modern. In a short time all went smoothly again.

Not since they shook hands had Elgar and Cecily encountered each other's glance. They looked at each other often, very often, but only when the look could not be returned; they exchanged not a syllable. Yet both knew that at some approaching moment, for them the supreme moment of this day, their eyes must meet. Not yet; not casually, and whilst others regarded them. The old ruins would be kind.

It was in the house of Meleager. They had walked among the coloured columns, and had visited the inner chamber, where upon the wall is painted the Judgment of Paris. Mr. Bradshaw passed out through the narrow doorway, and his voice was dulled;

Miriam passed with him, and, close after her, Mrs. Bradshaw. Reuben seemed to draw aside for Cecily, but she saw his hand extended towards her—it held a spray of maidenhair that he had just gathered. She took it, or would have taken it, but her hand was closed in his.

"I have stayed only to see you again," came panting from his lips. "I could not go till I had seen you again!"

And before the winged syllables had ceased, their eyes met; nor their eyes alone, for upon both was the constraint of passion that leaps like flame to its desire—mouth to mouth and heart to heart for one instant that concentrated all the joy of being.

What hand, centuries ago crumbled into indistinguishable dust, painted that parable of the youth making his award to Love? What eyes gazed upon it, when this was a home of man and woman, warm with life, listening all day long to the music of uttered thoughts? Dark-buried whilst so many ages of history went by, thrown open for the sunshine to rest upon its pallid antiquity, again had this chamber won a place in human hearts, witnessed the birth of joy and hope, blended itself with the destiny of mortals. He who pictured Paris dreamt not of these passionate lips and their unborn language, knew not that he wrought for a world hidden so far in time. Though his white-limbed goddess fade ghostlike, the symbol is as valid as ever. Did not her wan beauty smile youthful again in the eyes of these her latest worshippers?

And they went forth among the painted pillars, once more shunning each other's look. It was some minutes before Cecily knew that her fingers still crushed the spray of maidenhair; then she touched it gently, and secretly hid it within her glove. It must be dead by when she reached home, but that mattered nothing; would it not remain the sign of something deathless?

She believed so. In her vision the dead city had a new and wonderful life; it lay glorious in the light of heaven, its strait ways fit for the treading of divinities, its barren temples reconsecrate with song and sacrifice. She believed there was that within her soul which should survive all change and hazard—survive, it might be, even this warm flesh that it was hard not to think immortal.

She sought Miriam's side, took her hand, held it playfully as they walked on together.

"Why do you look at me so sadly, Miriam?"

"I did not mean to."

"Yet you do. Let me see you smile once—to-day."

But Miriam's smile was sadder than her grave look.

www.ingramcontent.com/pod-product-compliance
Lightning Source LLC
Chambersburg PA
CBHW031037120726
47905CB00007B/2220